Her Silent Knight

BELLES OF CHRISTMAS
FROST FAIR
BOOK 1

ASHTYN NEWBOLD

THREE LEAF
PUBLISHING

Edited by Jenny Proctor

Cover design by Ashtyn Newbold

Three Leaf Publishing, LLC

www.ashtynnewbold.com

❃ Created with Vellum

CHAPTER 1

✳

$\mathcal{N}$ever in all her days had Selina Ellis imagined she would set foot on the surface of the River Thames —at least not without sinking to the bottom.

Resting the toe of her boot on the uneven, icy surface, Selina strained her ears over the cacophony surrounding the Frost Fair, listening for the crack that would surely come as she trusted the ice with her weight. She took one step, then another, a smile stealing over her frigid cheeks. The crack didn't come. She wasn't falling between floating shards of ice. Here she was, standing on the Thames, halfway between London Bridge and Blackfriars. Somewhere deep below her feet was a body of water, one that would have caused her to sink only days before. A thrill shot through her bones at the phenomenon, and she walked farther across the ice, taking in the scene she had crossed town in a freezing carriage to experience.

Word of the Frost Fair had only been circulating town for a day, and already hundreds, if not thousands, were gathered on what Selina had heard called 'The City Road,' a walkway of sorts, spanning the entire distance between London Bridge and Black-friars Bridge. Flanking the walkway were booths, printing presses, and tradesmen of every sort, shouting out their offerings and selling them at thrice their previous value. Even Selina, much tighter with her purse than her elder sister, was tempted to purchase an item to prove she had been at the fair.

Fanciful women bundled from head to toe in wool coats, scarves, and hats encircled a nearby booth. Selina rose on her toes, catching sight of the fine jewelry on display in the center of the crowd.

Perhaps she could distract her mother with that.

"Selina, do be careful," Mama said in a stern voice. "We must stay close to the edge, should there happen to be an . . . accident." Mama held her skirts up with her gloved hands, taking minuscule steps to catch up to her daughter.

Selina turned, casting a pointed look near her mother's feet. "I suspect the edges to be the more dangerous terrain, Mama. Just yesterday I heard of a man and two young boys standing on the edge by London Bridge. The ice broke away and they would have been swept off had a waterman not come to their rescue."

Mama's features twisted in dismay, the outline of her face barely visible behind her scarf and cap. "And to think we have paid the watermen such a lofty fee to be here at all. And for what purpose?" She watched her feet again as she finally made it to Selina's side.

"To be daring. To experience a peculiarity. For a bit of frivolity." Selina smiled broadly, her gaze searching out the raucous noise coming from a booth nearby. Knock 'em downs, it appeared, was the cause of the noise. A group of gentlemen laughed as they played the game, and Selina was reminded of her *other* purpose in being here at the fair. Yes, the Frost Fair had sounded enticing, but none of the fair's attractions could compare to the attractions of Mr. Noah Skinner.

A sigh escaped her lips. What would he be wearing? He only owned one coat, but it was black, and there were a great number of men at the fair in black greatcoats. When she had arranged to meet him here, Selina had not expected the fair to attract *this* many people. Noah had told her he would be near the closest entrance to her home, which was the one she and her mother had taken. He had to be nearby—somewhere amid the immense crowd.

"Shall we purchase one of those reticules to prove we have come?" Selina pointed discreetly at a young woman walking by, a small silk bag in her hand, embroidered with the words, *Bought on the Thames.* If she could entice her mother to investigate the booth, Selina might be able to sneak away for a short time. Selina's gaze caught on another booth nearby, one with more exotic offerings, even a miniature statue of a tiger. She had always been fascinated with the animals. "Or we might purchase one of the little tigers." Selina pointed at the exotic booth.

"For the cost of a souvenir like that, we could each afford a new gown." Selina's mother tapped her fingers together. "And I have already spent a great deal of money on my preparations for Christmas. A paper from the press might be a wiser purchase, don't you think?"

After becoming a widow at a young age, Mama had been left with little to raise her daughters on and had never married again. Selina had heard tales of her father's estate and had even visited on one occasion, despite the fact that it had been entailed away to a distant relative. Mama had been cast away from all that she had married for. Her jointure was sufficient, although she liked to pretend to her daughters that they were far more needy than they truly were. And compared to the upbringing Mama had experienced, they *were* quite poor.

"A paper would be wiser, Mama," Selina said. "You are right. Shall we stand in line there first? Afterward, we might explore the rest of the city road so you might tell Mrs. Perry all that she has missed out on."

Mama's eyes gleamed a little at that suggestion. "Mrs. Perry *is* calling on us tomorrow afternoon, so I suppose she would like a firsthand account of the Frost Fair." Mama's steps no longer seemed quite so tentative as she followed Selina to the back of the line at the nearest printing press.

Selina smiled at her small victory. She knew her mother so well. There was an unspoken rivalry between Mama and Mrs. Perry, one that could only come from being neighbors for nearly twenty years, both with two daughters of similar ages and fortunes. It was a constant competition over whose daughters were prettier, whose would be married first, and whose would be married to the highest-ranking gentleman. Rose, Selina's elder sister, had married into wealth, but not title. That was Selina's duty if Mama were to claim victory over Mrs. Perry and her one married daughter—who had wed a man of at least one thousand more per year than Rose's husband.

And that was precisely why Mama could not know about Mr. Noah Skinner, and especially not the fact that he was waiting for Selina somewhere on the surface of the River Thames.

Selina cast her gaze about the nearby booths, searching for

the dark hair and broad shoulders she knew belonged to Noah. Her heart leaped when she caught sight of his familiar face. He stood near a tent where the open door revealed several people dancing the reel within, while others sipped on hot tea, the steam rising visibly in the cold.

Noah's gaze found hers, and a charming smile stole over his lips. He took one step toward her, but she gestured at her mother, who was distracted by the booth ahead. He nodded in understanding, retreating to the tent.

Before Mama could have the chance to turn around, Selina took off across the ice, careful not to trip on the rugged surface. She glanced back, relieved to find Mama's gaze still transfixed on the workings of the printing press.

Noah stood with his arm outstretched, and the moment Selina reached him, he took her hand, pulling her quickly behind the tent where her mother couldn't see them. As any gentleman would, he released his grip on her hand the moment they were tucked safely away from the crowd.

Disappointment dropped through her stomach. She enjoyed the warmth of his fingers, even through their gloves. He did not need to always act like a *gentleman*. Anyone in society would neglect to call him one, no matter his behavior. He was the son of a solicitor. *Her family's* solicitor. And that posed a problem no amount of gentlemanly behavior could rectify in the eyes of her mother.

"Dear Selina." Noah searched her gaze, his deep brown eyes warming her insides like a cup of hot tea. "I have missed you."

As his eyes searched her face, she carefully touched her blonde curls, ensuring they still hung from the outside of her cap. Despite the lack of propriety, she had worn her hair down, hoping it would aid in keeping her neck warm. She had seen a few other ladies at the fair with the same style.

"I—I have missed you too," she said. There was something about Noah that made her infuriatingly bashful. He was simply too charming for her words to function properly.

"How long have you been waiting?" Selina asked in a quiet voice. "My mother was quite afraid to come to the fair, or I would have been here sooner."

He cocked his head to one side, a slow smile spreading on his lips. "Were you truly so eager to see me that you would convince your fear-stricken mother to accompany you?"

"She is not so fearful now." Selina avoided directly answering his question. "She is actually quite eager to tell our neighbor, Mrs. Perry, of her experience here."

"Women are always searching for something to boast of." He smiled, his tall frame shifting slightly forward as he searched her eyes. "I wish it were possible for you to boast of me."

He did not need to explain for Selina to know what he meant. They were forced to hide their courtship from her mother, who would wholeheartedly disapprove.

"If my mother knew you, she would have plenty to boast of." Selina tipped her head up to look at him, taking in all the things that recommended him. He was very handsome, he was very . . . flattering to her. Very . . .

She bit her lip. She would have to compile a better list than that if she were to try to convince her mother to allow her to marry him. She did not know him well enough for that yet, but she did know that she was in love with him. He was far more attentive than any gentleman she knew, and she had never felt more important than when she was with him. She loved him far more than Rose loved her husband, and far more than Mama had loved Selina's father. Selina would rather marry the son of a solicitor than someone she would become 'fond of' over the years as her mother had promised. She'd claimed there was no reason to aspire to *love.*

Noah smiled down at her, and a flutter erupted in her stomach. Yes, he was quite handsome, indeed. "You must tell your mother of me eventually, you know." The intensity of his gaze was somewhat shocking, and she felt as if she couldn't refuse his request even if she wanted to.

"My mother loves Christmastime." Selina interlocked her fingers in front of her. "There will be no better time to tell her than the holidays." It was already the nineteenth of December. How could Selina gather the courage to tell her mother by the end of the month? Perhaps she could extend her confession to Twelfth Night. It wasn't that she feared her mother's disappointment—she had faced enough of *that* throughout her life to be accustomed to it. It was that she feared her mother would find a way to stop her.

"What shall we do if your mother disapproves?" Noah appeared genuinely distressed, removing his hat for a moment to rake a hand over his thick, dark hair.

An idea flitted through Selina's head, but she didn't dare say it aloud.

Noah seemed to read her mind—or her expression. "We could marry in secret," he whispered, a sly smile on his lips.

Selina's stomach flipped, her hands perspiring in her gloves. The flush his words had caused on her skin made her feel warm all over, despite her standing on a sheet of thick ice. "An elopement?"

Noah paused as a couple walked past, waiting until they were out of earshot to continue speaking. "If it is the only way we can be together, I would not object. Would you?"

Selina shook her head, which had become very light. "Not at all."

Noah smiled, taking both her hands in his and tugged her into an abrupt embrace. His arms wrapped around her waist. She froze, a mixture of shock and excitement pulsing through her veins.

Had she just become *engaged* atop the River Thames?

Surely Mrs. Perry's daughters could not live up to that.

Noah held her tightly, squeezing as though he never meant to let go. "I am so pleased to hear that," he muttered, pulling back to look at her face. "No matter the obstacles, we shall find our happiness together."

Selina smiled, clinging to his upper arms as she looked up at him. The realization hit her that they were standing at a very public gathering, where any watchful eyes would meet their recent embrace with suspicion.

Selina's gaze darted to the right, and panic cut through her happy, unexpected moment.

Standing just a few feet away was a man with yet another familiar face, one that took her several seconds to recognize.

A face she had not seen in three years.

But she would recognize the black curls, crystal blue eyes, and towering build of Edmund Sharp anywhere.

CHAPTER 2

*E*ven after blinking three times, the image was the same.

A young woman, with her blonde hair hanging loose about her shoulders, held tightly to the arms of a gentleman, one whom she had just been even closer to moments before. It could have been a married couple, and the embrace could have even been proper since Edmund did not know many people in London. But something had stopped him in his tracks.

He blinked a fourth time to clear his vision enough to confirm that the young woman was not a stranger.

Miss Selina Ellis, her blonde curls much longer than he remembered, her cheeks much redder, stared at him with wide blue eyes. In an instant, she jumped away from the man in whose arms she had just quite happily been. She was the very image of guilt. Edmund might have believed that she was married, even at her young age, if she hadn't just jumped away from her suitor as if the ice had cracked between them.

For a long moment, Selina and Edmund simply stared at each other, until Edmund cleared his throat. He could have pretended that he hadn't seen anything if Selina's blue eyes hadn't captured his attention so thoroughly. No matter how awkward the situation was becoming, he couldn't seem to look away.

Selina crossed her arms, turning away from the mysterious man beside her. Edmund's trance broke long enough for him to examine the gentleman. Tall, dark hair, dark eyes, and a smile that screamed of mischief.

Lud . . . Edmund recognized *him*, too. A sudden surge of protectiveness washed over Edmund's shoulders, and he leveled the man with a glare. What the devil was a genteel young woman like Selina doing with Skinner? Where was her chaperone?

"Miss Ellis," Edmund said, finally gaining control of his voice. He bowed in her direction, rising to meet her gaze once again. He hadn't expected to ever meet any member of the Ellis family again but here stood Miss Selina, seemingly quite uncomfortable with the current situation. She lifted her chin, tempting him to question her. He cleared his throat again, searching for the right words. Was she in danger?

Surely she was if Mr. Noah Skinner was nearby.

Distaste rose in Edmund's throat, and he swallowed hard.

"Miss Ellis," he repeated, pretending he hadn't seen anything out of the ordinary—at least for now. "I did not know your family was still in London."

Her skin had turned rather pale compared to the pink flush her cheeks had carried when she had first seen Edmund. "Mr. Sharp." She lowered into a quick curtsy. "My family is always in London." Her voice was barely above a whisper. "My mother

10

never wishes to leave. As I recall, you despise your visits to London."

Edmund looked down at his boots before glancing up again. She was right; London was the last place he would ever wish to be, especially now that his grandmother was gone. But the ten-day journey he had taken to get to London to see his grandmother before her death had been slowed by a heavy snowstorm. Then another, and another. The blasted River Thames had even frozen over. And his grandmother had died before he could make it up her front steps.

He let out a sigh. "Well, despite that, I am here, and likely will be until the frost thaws enough for the roads to be traveled safely. I came to the fair as a way to pass the time."

"I see." She kicked softly at the ice before turning to face Skinner. She whispered something Edmund couldn't hear before Skinner took a step forward, stopping in front of Edmund with a bow. He didn't speak a word, but his eyes cast Edmund something of a warning before he lost himself in the crowd on the opposite side of the dancing tent.

With Skinner's departure, Selina appeared relieved, at least to some extent. She wrung her hands together. "I suppose I should explain why I was with that gentleman. He—"

"He is not a gentleman." Edmund shook his head.

Her eyes flashed, color returning to her cheeks. "You do not know him."

"Mr. Noah Skinner. The son of Mr. George Skinner, the solicitor employed by both your family and mine." Edmund took a step closer. "I know him, Miss Ellis, but I wish I did not."

Her brow furrowed. "Have you elevated yourself so much in

your absence that you would regret to know a man beneath your station?"

"It is not his station that concerns me. It is his character." Edmund exhaled sharply, sending a puff of fog into the air. He did not wish to argue with Selina already. She was a kind girl —*woman*—if not a bit naive. Unfortunately, that quality seemed to have increased over the last three years. Could he blame her? Skinner was a master of deception.

Selina let out a quiet laugh. "You are not in a position to be concerned about me. At any rate, you are a foot soldier. You are barely above Mr. Skinner in rank, and if he finds success in his trade, he may even exceed you in fortune. So please, Mr. Sharp, do not look down your nose at him a moment longer."

"Sir Edmund."

Her pale eyebrows rose. "Pardon me?"

"That is how you ought to address me now. We have both grown up a little since our last meeting. I have come to make good decisions, enough to earn me the honor of becoming a knight; on the contrary, you, in secretly courting the son of your family's solicitor, have clearly come to make poor ones. I am glad to have found you here today so I might put an end to these clandestine meetings before you discover Mr. Skinner's true character for yourself." Edmund turned around, searching the crowds beyond the tent. She must have brought her mother or sister with her.

"I love him!" Selina blurted. "He is not without fault, but neither are you, nor me, nor anyone."

"You do not deny that you are secretly courting him?"

She tugged on the sides of her blue coat. "It is not a traditional courtship . . ."

"Devil take it," Edmund muttered, exhaling through compressed lips. She appeared suddenly bashful, small, as if she had finally realized the extent of her wrongdoing.

She glanced up at Edmund from under her lashes, her voice tentative. "Please, do not tell my mother. My happiness depends on my future with Mr. Skinner."

In truth, her happiness depended on a future *without* him. Edmund studied her for a long moment. What could Skinner's motivations be in courting her? In the past, he had often been heard boasting of his ability to woo any woman he chose. Was her beauty all that had drawn him to her? Selina had always been beautiful, but she had no fortune, and Skinner had never planned to work for his money with anything but charming words and smiles. Could his motivation really be love? Or did he have a more sinister purpose in pursuing Selina? An ache had begun spreading behind Edmund's eyes. He had to help her. The trouble was, she did not want to be helped. That was clear by the way she stood with her feet planted and arms crossed.

"I cannot betray Mrs. Ellis by not revealing this information to her. Your reputation could depend on it. I know it is not my place to censure you for your behavior, but the fact that you are behaving in this way is an insult to your upbringing."

Selina glared at him, much like she had when they were children and the top of her head only reached the middle of his waistcoat. Now her head nearly reached his chin, and her glare sliced through him much sharper than before. "I have always believed there is wisdom in being led through life by my heart. There are some, including you and my mother, who would disagree. All the training that has taught me to pursue a match of wealth and consequence has only been motivated by greed and boastfulness. If I were to marry Mr. Skinner, I would be nothing. But I would rather be *nothing* and happy than *something* and filled with regret for the rest of my life." Her defensive tone sent Edmund back a step.

"Are you only courting him to defy your mother?" he asked with a scoff. "To make a point?"

"I told you, I love him."

"Do you love him, or do you love the notion of marrying him?"

Selina huffed a breath. "I'm afraid I do not understand your meaning."

She was determined, that much was certain. Edmund crossed his arms over his chest. "If you are going to demand my silence on the subject of your secret courtship, then you will have to answer all of my questions."

Her eyes lit up with hope. "You will not tell my mother?"

The knot in Edmund's stomach refused to leave. He had always prided himself on his ability to sense when something was wrong. And there were too many things to count that were wrong with Selina courting Skinner. He couldn't stand by and allow her to make such a mistake. His family and hers had been friends for years, and he wouldn't be able to rest if he knew he had allowed something like this to happen right under his nose.

But he couldn't bring himself to betray Selina either, not with her staring up at him with her large blue eyes filled with worry and desperation. An idea struck him as he remembered that there was nothing he could do to stop himself from being trapped in London for Christmastide. Before today, he had envisioned himself spending the holidays alone in his townhouse, checking the windows for any sign of melting snow every five minutes. But now he saw a purpose much more worthy of his time.

"I will grant your request," Edmund said, "if you will grant mine."

Selina's round eyes filled with confusion, and she bit her lower lip. "I suppose that is fair." She tipped her head to one side. "I do not have money to pay you for your silence."

Edmund couldn't stop his smile at the ridiculousness of her offer, though it confirmed the fact that Skinner could not have been pursuing her for any financial gain. "I am not asking for money. I am asking for . . . hospitality."

The furrow on her brow only deepened.

"I will be trapped in London until the roads are clear, and with my grandmother's death, I have no relatives with whom to spend Christmastide. Rather than endure the holidays alone, I would request an invitation to spend them at your family's home."

Selina's jaw lowered slightly, and her nose scrunched. Edmund held back his smile. He hadn't expected her to be pleased with the arrangement.

"Why do you wish to stay with us? You seem the sort who would enjoy his solitude."

Edmund did all he could to evade suspicion, putting on an expression of innocence similar to the one Selina wore. Except his was more convincing. "It has been far too long since I enjoyed a true country Christmas, and I know how your mother carries on the traditions she learned from her upbringing in Yorkshire." He smiled. "It really is a small favor to request for my silence on such a shocking discovery as I made today." He may have been doing it too brown, but she seemed to believe his act.

"My mother *has* always adored you." Selina looked up at him as if she were trying to ascertain *why*, exactly, her mother would ever like him. "She would be overjoyed to have you as a guest." She gave a weak smile. "As would I if you will keep your word."

Edmund smiled. "You have my silence."

She eyed him again, her suspicion slowly fading. How could she have been so suspicious of him and not of Skinner? Was he that much better at acting than Edmund? Perhaps it was because Selina had known Edmund as a child, and many of his expressions were likely the same. She could read him more easily, just as he could read her.

And he could tell—she was not in love with Skinner.

She possibly believed she was, but a young woman would not appear as she had today if she were in love. She wouldn't be stiff and uncertain when released from the arms of the man she loved. Whether Selina realized it or not, she was nothing more than intrigued by the man. Perhaps attracted to him. She may have even enjoyed his company. But love, real, abiding love, was something Selina had not experienced before, and as stubborn as she was, that kind of love was the only thing that could ever convince her to leave Skinner behind.

Edmund had promised his silence, but living within the same walls as Selina for the next several weeks provided its own opportunity to protect her from Skinner and whatever his secret motives entailed. Edmund couldn't sit back and watch her marry him. Though no small part of him wondered if it might be better for Selina if he simply told her family the truth now, rather than subject her to the plans presently hatching in his mind.

Without a doubt, she would come to regret their bargain.

CHAPTER 3

❄

Selina had never known Edmund to have anything resembling mischief in his countenance, but what else could she call that gleam in his eyes? She searched his face for a long moment. What had she just agreed to? Was it really worth having him in her house through the new year, or perhaps even longer?

It certainly wasn't worth discovering the meaning behind that mischievous expression of his. Regret burrowed into her chest, but she pushed it away. What other choice did she have?

"I thank you for your promise, Sir Edmund." Selina tried to smile, but her cheeks were too cold. "May I ask one more thing of you?"

He raised one dark eyebrow. "Yes."

When had he become so . . . old? No, old wasn't the right description. He was still in his twenties, but he no longer looked like a boy or even what one would call a young man. He was a man. A plain man. Well, not plain; he was far more handsome than what could ever be considered fair, with his dark curls, blue eyes, and distinct jawline.

Selina cleared her thoughts, focusing on the request she meant to make. "I imagine, at this moment, that my mother is frantically searching for me. If you would be so kind as to escort me back to her, she will not be permitted to scold me in your presence, nor would she wish to. I daresay at the sight of you she will be all pleasantries and smiles. She may even forget she wished to ring me a fine peal."

Edmund chuckled, a deep vibration sounding through his chest. "And she might just invite me to stay for the holidays without you having a hand in it at all."

"If you act pitiful enough, then I'm sure she will." Selina hadn't meant her words to be harsh, but Edmund seemed surprised by them, nonetheless.

"My circumstances here in London *are* slightly pitiful." He shrugged one shoulder. "But there is nothing I can do to change them." Extending his arm to Selina, they began walking away from the tent and across the ice. Shouting and laughter filled the frigid air, and in her time behind the tent, Selina noticed a fire had been lit, where a sheep was being roasted for one of the nearby eating booths.

"Why are you here in London at all?" she asked.

"I wished to see my grandmother before her death, as she specifically requested my company. My travels were delayed by the snow, and she died before I could arrive."

Selina pressed a hand to her chest. "Oh, dear. I am very sorry to hear that." Selina had fond memories of Edmund's grandmother. Each time he came to London when they were children, she brought him for a visit. Edmund would spend his days in whatever activities Selina and her sister could invent while his grandmother sat in the drawing room with Mama, embroidering or discussing distant places. If Selina remembered correctly, his grandmother had been fond of travel.

"It was disappointing." Edmund spoke with a smile as though to buoy up his spirits with the false expression. "At least I was able to assist in the funeral proceedings. I think she would be glad I am staying in London for Christmas."

Selina suddenly didn't feel so bad about hosting Edmund for the holidays. He deserved *free* hospitality after all he had endured. He could have asked for much more in exchange for his silence. But there was one thing that worried her the most about his presence in her home. Mama adored him, and he bore a title. Not one as significant as earl or viscount or even baron, but with the knighthood combined with Edmund's character, Mama would stop at nothing to secure him for her daughter. Selina could already hear her mother's gleeful voice: *Lady Sharp—could there ever be a finer name?*

Selina glanced at the booth where she had left her mother but found no sign of her. Had she abandoned the line when she noticed Selina was missing? Selina moved her feet faster across the ice, pulling slightly against her grip on Edmund's arm. They passed a group of women huddled together, and after checking each of their faces, Selina confirmed that her mother was not among them. In a fair filled with hundreds of people, her mother could be anywhere. Glancing left and right, she marched across the ice without a bit of the nervousness she had experienced when first setting foot on the river. She nearly forgot she was on ice at all.

And that was the problem.

Before she could catch her balance, her right foot slipped out from under her, the movement so sudden that the same occurred to her left foot. She clutched Edmund's arm, crashing down with all her weight as he lost his footing as well. Edmund hit the ground first, falling onto his back. Selina landed with a thud . . .

. . . on top of him.

The front of her head struck his shoulder as she landed, and her head spun for a moment before his face came into view. Much too close to hers. He wore a grimace similar to her own. Propping himself up on one elbow, he placed one hand on Selina's waist. For a fleeting moment, Selina thought he was trying to keep her there, laying against him, but she realized he was helping her sit up. Her cheeks flamed as she noticed the spectators that had turned to watch the scene, amusement readily upon their faces, some of whom appeared so intrigued, they might even call this the most entertaining scene at the fair. A sharp pain pricked at Selina's scalp as she moved, and she glanced down to see one long lock of her hair wrapped around the first button of Edmund's coat.

"Wait," she whispered through her teeth, cringing as the hair pulled again.

Edmund glanced down at his coat. Selina sat halfway on the ice, halfway on Edmund's legs as she struggled to find her balance enough to free her hands. Edmund had already begun working on untangling her hair. He cursed under his breath before tugging off his gloves with his teeth, setting to work at it again. He seemed to have noticed the spectators as well.

When several seconds passed, which felt far more like an eternity, a high-pitched voice met her ears.

"Selina! What are you doing?" Mama stood above them, her eyes round with shock.

Selina glanced up without moving her head. Thankfully, Edmund managed to untangle her hair, brushing it back onto her shoulder before clearing his throat awkwardly. Selina wriggled off his legs, too embarrassed to meet his gaze or take his hand as she scrambled to her feet. She brushed the rest of the hair away from her eyes before correcting her posture. She prayed the red on her cheeks could be excused for the cold. "Mama," she breathed, swallowing hard. "Sir Edmund was escorting me back to you when we slipped on the ice."

"Sir Ed—" Mama's voice cut off when she looked behind Selina, her expression lifting at the sight of Edmund, who was brushing snow off the back of his coat. When he noticed her keen gaze, he bowed in her direction, confirming Selina's statement.

Selina's shoulders slumped with relief. She had known he would soften Mama's heart.

"It would seem my arm is not as stable as I thought." Edmund exchanged a glance with Selina before casting Mama a broad smile, which brought the same expression instantly to her face.

"Oh, Sir Edmund! I am so pleased to see you in London again. What has brought you to town? And in this weather? How long have you been here without calling on us?" She arched one accusatory eyebrow at him.

He chuckled, and Selina could hardly believe the way her mother seemed to have already forgotten the fact that she had just found them in a very uncomfortable situation. The color of Edmund's eyes flashed through her mind again. They had been quite close to hers just moments before. The ice had made them appear much closer to grey than blue.

As Edmund explained to Selina's mother all his reasoning for being in London, Selina brushed the bits of ice off her skirts, trying not to relive her humiliation. Where was Noah? Had he seen her fall? The idea set her cheeks flaming all over again.

"Well, I am glad you were here to bring my daughter back to me." Mama's voice interrupted Selina's thoughts. "I thought she had fallen through the ice somewhere." She shot Selina a look of reprimand, but it was overshadowed by a lingering smile. "Oh, Sir Edmund, we are *so* very pleased you are in town."

Selina refrained from letting out an exasperated sigh. Why could Noah never receive such admiration from Mama? No matter what he did, he would never be greeted so warmly.

"I did not plan to be here so long," Edmund said. "With the frost, I don't know when it will be safe to travel home."

"Do you have plans for Christmastide?"

"Not at present."

Mama gasped. "We would be delighted if you would stay with us for the holidays. I have been quite starved of guests during these cold months."

Edmund threw Selina a sidelong glance, a slight smirk on his lips for only her to see. "That is very kind of you to offer, and I would be a fool to refuse. I have heard of your enthusiasm for the holiday." He smiled, and Mama clapped her hands together, her thick wool gloves muffling the sound.

"Did you hear that, Selina? Sir Edmund has agreed to stay with us for Christmastide. Is that not delightful? The two of you may enjoy reflecting on your childhood memories of one another whilst keeping warm by the fire."

"That sounds delightful," Edmund said.

Selina did not recall any memories of Edmund worth reflecting on. At least not any that wouldn't end in an argument. Most of her memories of him involved him standing silently by his grandmother's side, whispering to her of his wishes to return home. He'd never spoken to Selina much on his visits until he'd grown older and learned how to converse without shyness. Now he seemed a little too opposite of shy. A little too mischievous for her liking. What did he mean by that smirk? Each time his gaze flitted to her, it sprung up on his lips again. He must have known she wasn't fond of the idea of him staying so long at her family's home.

Stop, Selina, she scolded herself. He had been quite respectful in agreeing to keep her secret. There was no reason she should dread his presence in the home. He was kind and good, if not a little irksome in his opinions. He deserved to enjoy a lovely Christmastide. They needn't spend any time together outside of Mama's planned activities. She could still go about her life as usual. Breakfast at ten, reading by the fire until taking tea with Mama and the occasional visitor in the early afternoon, and then a solo visit to Miss Brisbane's. Well, at least her *mother* thought Selina visited Miss Brisbane.

In truth, Selina and Noah had made a habit of meeting outside his father's office during that time, when his father was away on calls. He always entertained her with the most exciting conversation. And now they had a marriage to make arrangements for.

She nearly sighed. Nothing could interfere with her happiness now. She was *secretly engaged.* Not even the Frost Fair was as thrilling as that.

"Well, now that we are all together again, shall we explore more of the fair?" Mama asked. "I never did purchase my souvenir. After I do, I should be pleased to return home and ready the house for your arrival, Sir Edmund."

Selina exchanged a glance with Edmund, who gave a polite smile. He was enjoying this far too much. Mama walked ahead on the ice, surprisingly unafraid, even after seeing Selina and Edmund's fall.

When Mama was several paces away, Edmund leaned closer to Selina, speaking in a whisper. "Let us hope Mr. Skinner did not see that."

He didn't even need to explain what *that* was. Selina's face still burned at the thought of their fall. Edmund smiled, and the expression was still just as surprising as it had been the first time she had seen it.

She eyed him with suspicion. "I believe you wish he *had* seen it."

His eyes rounded innocently as he extended his arm to her. "Why would I wish for that?"

Edmund couldn't pretend he was now *supporting* her match with Noah. There was something very wrong with his smirk. Not even Christmastide could make a serious boy like Edmund smile so much.

Not a *boy,* she reminded herself. Though when she took his heavily muscled arm, she doubted she would ever need to remind herself again. She wanted to ask why he disliked Noah so much, but she didn't want Edmund to think she was doubting her suitor. She wasn't. Noah had proven himself trustworthy in their time spent together.

Edmund, however, had not.

His dark lashes fluttered and his gaze dropped to hers, but she looked away fast. The less of his face she saw, the better, for it had become far too handsome.

CHAPTER 4

❄

*R*ubbing his finger across the smudge on Grandmother's silver elephant statue did not serve to clean it. Edmund slid it across the table with a sigh. She would have never allowed it to be left so dirty.

He glanced up at the portrait of his grandparents that hung above the sofa in the drawing room. Grandmother, so regal, even with that no-nonsense glint in her eye. After being left a widow, she had only softened for a small group of people. Edmund had been privileged to be one of them.

The house was empty and quiet. Without her humming, he could hear the clock ticking. The chair in which she had always sat was still sunken slightly in the middle. The sight brought a weak smile to Edmund's face. Though he would have much preferred to see the chair occupied, at least she had left her mark upon it.

He glanced at the elephant statue on the side table one more time. She had traveled to India after her husband's death, and she had never ceased to tell Edmund tales of all her adventures there. They had shared a love of the grand animals, and he had been especially fascinated by elephants as a child.

He would have taken the statue from the side table as a way to remember his Grandmother, but there was a slight problem. He hadn't received word of her will.

The story Grandmother was most fond of was how she had purchased her London home with her own money, and that she could give it, along with her entire fortune, to whomever she chose. It did induce her grandchildren to behave a little better while they were visiting. Edmund's older brother had inherited their family home, and Grandmother had not been as fond of her granddaughters as her grandsons. So that left Edmund as a very likely beneficiary.

But he had heard nothing. There was much the severe weather had delayed in London, but he had assumed he would have heard from Grandmother's solicitor by now.

Turning his back on the statue, he took a deep breath. As much as he would have liked to, he was not spending Christmastide with Grandmother this year, or ever again. He was spending it with the Ellises, and they were expecting him that afternoon. Tomorrow was the first St. Thomas's Day in years that Grandmother hadn't used her status as a widow to receive gifts from all her neighbors.

He checked his pocket watch. There was still time to stop by the solicitor's office on his way to inquire about any arrangements Grandmother might have made with Mr. Skinner before her death. Thankfully, the elder Mr. Skinner was much more agreeable than his son. And trustworthy.

How did Selina not see her suitor for what he was? Even if

Skinner did have true feelings for her, what was she thinking courting a man so far beneath her station? As beautiful as she was, she could have her pick of men. She was barely out in society; she hadn't even *tried* to find a different match. How could she call what she felt for Skinner love if she didn't have anything else to compare it to? He shushed his thoughts. All they had done was cause him frustration.

When the last of the belongings he had brought to London were packed, he took the coach across town, shivering slightly as he sat inside. The roads were covered in thick ice, so the coach moved much slower than usual. The bursting of water pipes had caused the abundance of ice on the roads. Edmund had heard a rumor that a man had been challenged to skate from Long Acre to St. James's Park in five minutes and had completed the task. It seemed the entirety of London, and not just the River Thames, had been fully frosted over.

When the coach finally stopped in front of Skinner's office, Edmund stepped carefully down to the road, sliding his feet rather than stepping to avoid another fall. A brisk, cold wind blew at his hat, and he barely stopped it from falling as he stepped through the door.

A tall clerk with greying hair stepped out of a nearby door to greet him.

"I wish to speak with Mr. Skinner," Edmund said. "Is he available?"

The clerk shook his head. "I'm afraid not." He eyed the door behind Edmund, which had failed to close all the way. Edmund could hardly feel his own hands and feet, so he certainly hadn't felt the chill that had likely begun spreading in the warm office.

He reached back to close the door before regarding the clerk again. "Does he have a moment this afternoon to speak with me? I have just a few brief questions."

The clerk's thin lips were stiff and straight. "No, I'm afraid he will be out of his office for quite some time now. He left a fortnight ago, shortly before the frost set in. The roads won't be safe to travel for weeks. I extend the sincerest of apologies on his behalf for the delay in service. Please take his card and return when the snow has begun to melt."

Edmund frowned. "Could I write to him with my question? It is a simple one pertaining to my grandmother, Mrs. Sharp's, will."

"You could, indeed, but even the mail is quite slow. Mr. Skinner has left much of his work to his son in his absence, who should be able to assist you on simple matters. Shall I send him down to speak with you?"

Before Edmund had a chance to refuse, the younger Mr. Skinner's voice, deep and grating, met his ears from down the hallway. It seemed he had been listening for the opportune moment to present himself. "Sir Edmund, how do you do?"

Edmund turned, hiding his grimace at the sight of Skinner and his over-confident stride. How much did Selina not know about him? Did she know he was known among men for his gambling and known among women for his rakish behavior? How many rumors had escaped Selina's ears in her short time out in society? That could have been why she was Mr. Skinner's target. She hadn't yet been advised to run away as fast as she could.

"I am well, and you?" Edmund squared his shoulders, keeping his words polite, but with great effort.

Skinner looked upward and let out a contented sigh.

"Quite." His gaze shifted to Edmund again. "Come to my office and I will try to assist you with any questions you have regarding your grandmother's will."

Edmund almost refused but stopped himself. He *did* have several questions for Mr. Skinner, none of which had anything to do with the will.

Edmund followed him to a doorway down the hall, taking the armchair in front of the solicitor's desk, which was extremely cluttered, likely due to its current occupant. Skinner slumped down in the seat behind the desk which he had positioned to partially face the large hearth. Warmth radiated from the fire, filling the room with a little too much heat to be comfortable. Edmund's fingers uncurled from his palms.

"It was an interesting coincidence to see you at the Frost Fair yesterday," Skinner said in an offhand voice. "You seemed quite familiar with Miss Ellis."

"Not as familiar as you did," Edmund said.

Skinner froze for a moment before laughing, propping his elbows on the table. "What did your fanciful imagination manage to deduce from what you observed at the fair?"

"Miss Ellis told me you are courting her in secret."

"She *told* you, or you made that assumption?"

"Both."

Skinner sighed, a flash of irritation in his eyes. "She told you, despite our agreement not to tell anyone. Women are always far too eager when they have an opportunity of marriage before them." He smiled, but the irritation still lingered in his expression. Edmund's suspicions only intensified. Skinner did not love Selina. The only things he loved were money and brandy. Which again begged the question: why was he courting her at all?

"Surely Miss Ellis could find another opportunity of marriage, should it present itself." Edmund kept his gaze fixed on Skinner. "Why has she set her sights on you?"

"I have always possessed the skill of attracting women." Skinner locked his fingers together with a smile.

"Why have you chosen to marry her? Wouldn't you seek an heiress if you are so skilled?" Edmund watched for any sign of dismay in Skinner's expression, for any sign that he was appalled at the suggestion, but he wasn't. He seemed . . . amused instead.

"She is a very attractive young woman, and that is all that drew me to her at first. Then I came to find myself very much in love with her. Even without her money, I would be smitten."

"I do not believe you."

Skinner laughed under his breath. "I do not need you to believe me. I need you to promise that you will keep our secret."

"Miss Ellis has already asked that much of me, and for *her,* I will oblige."

Skinner chuckled again, straightening a stack of papers on his desk.

Edmund sat back against his chair for a brief moment before Skinner's words caught up to him. His spine straightened. "Even without her *money?*"

"Pardon me?"

"You said you would be smitten even without Miss Ellis's money." Edmund frowned. "Selina does not have a dowry."

"There are certain things you discover as you peruse the files on your father's desk, Sir Edmund. Miss Ellis's mother may not have been able to afford an inheritance for her daughter, but her childless uncle and aunt in Cheshire certainly have. Mrs. Ellis has been aware of this for months but is waiting to tell her daughter as a way to usher in the new year with good fortune." He chuckled. "Once Selina learns of her fortune, she will never realize I already knew. And I daresay I have stolen enough of her heart that she would not care even if she did."

Edmund crossed his arms, shaking his head. It all made sense now. An heiress would suspect a fortune hunter in an instant when pursued by Skinner. But a naive young woman with a fortune unbeknownst to her? The perfect target.

"You know I cannot keep your intentions from her," Edmund warned. "She deserves to know."

Skinner seemed unaffected by Edmund's words, picking up a paper from his stack before Edmund could see the front. "I also found this document, which appears to be the last will and testament of Frederica Hester Sharp. Does that name sound familiar?"

Edmund stiffened as Mr. Skinner turned abruptly in his chair toward the hearth. In one motion, he thrust his arm out and hovered Edmund's grandmother's will dangerously close to the flames.

Edmund stood, afraid to make another move with the corner of the paper so close to catching fire. One flick of Skinner's wrist and it would be gone forever.

Skinner's eyes darted between Edmund and the flames. "If you tell Selina—or anyone else—any detail of our conversation today, I will burn this document. If she expresses any doubts to me about my motivations or changes her mind about marrying me, and I discover you were responsible, you will never see this will again." Skinner moved the paper impossibly closer to the flames. "Stay out of business that is not your own, and I will do the same." Skinner nodded toward the paper, his expression growing serious.

Heat climbed Edmund's neck, and he curled his fists. He had been right about Skinner. He was manipulative and cunning, and love was the last thing he would ever give. All he did was take. And he had taken poor Selina's heart with no intention of truly giving his in return . . . at least not without a steep price.

Edmund's determination to protect Selina rose as he took a step away from the desk. "I won't say a word." His voice was hard.

"Good. Then I will keep this will safe until my father's return." Skinner slipped the document back into his stack before gesturing at the door behind Edmund. "I wish you a good day."

Edmund didn't wish Skinner the same as he walked out the door. He had never been so eager to step outside in the frigid weather than he was now.

Anger pulsed through his veins as he climbed back into the coach. What Skinner didn't know was that Edmund was going to be the Ellises' guest over the next several weeks, and Edmund planned to keep him unaware of that fact. No one would be closer to Selina than Edmund. Skinner didn't know that Edmund could keep silent *and* still stop Selina from marrying him at the same time. All it would take was a little creativity.

CHAPTER 5

❄

"Might I ask where you are you going?"

The question came from behind as Selina grasped the front door handle. Drat. *Drat, drat, drat.* She turned around with an innocent expression, her heart beating fast against her ribs. As expected, Edmund stood with one elbow leaning against the banister, a deep arch in his right eyebrow.

"I visit my dear friend Miss Brisbane at this time every day." She smiled to reassure him before turning back toward the door.

Four clicks of Edmund's boots sounded on the marble floor. She scowled and whirled to face him just as he reached for the door handle. She froze, trapped between Edmund and the door. She assumed he would move, given their sudden proximity, but he stayed still, tipping his head down to look at her with no small measure of suspicion. "I happen to know *Mrs.* Brisbane has a cold and is not accepting visitors in her house until she recovers." His voice was deep and certain, his eyes cutting into Selina like two shards of ice.

"I-I am an exception. I am always welcome." Selina tipped her head up, exuding all the confidence she could. In reality, she was not aware of an illness in the Brisbane household, and she hadn't visited Miss Brisbane in weeks.

Good heavens, why wouldn't Edmund back up a step? Her heart pounded at his closeness and her palms began to perspire in her gloves. She hadn't put on all this heavy wool just to stand inside, trapped between Edmund and the door.

"Would a young lady wear rouge on her lips to visit a female friend?" Edmund's gaze flitted to her lips for a brief moment before meeting her gaze again with that blasted arched eyebrow.

Selina's cheeks heated even more. How inappropriate could his questions be? Infuriating man! Simply because their families were friends and they had known each other as children did not mean he could behave so . . . *comfortably* around her, asking questions that were none of his concern.

"A lady always tries to look her best." Selina leveled him with her gaze. "And behave in a manner that is proper." Her words were pointed at him but didn't seem to have the desired effect. If anything, he moved closer, peeling back her facade—it seemed—with his gaze.

"Is sneaking away to have a tête-a-tête with a man considered proper behavior?"

"I already told you, I am visiting Miss Brisbane." Selina felt a pang of guilt at her lies. She might have told him the truth if he hadn't been so accusatory and condescending. When had he decided to act as if she were his ward? Her father had died just before she was born. She had already made it to the age of eighteen without needing to be protected, so why did Edmund think he could do so now?

After a long moment, he seemed to relent, stepping back. Selina exhaled, unsettled by her reaction to him. The space between them was still small, but at least there was *space.*

"Considering the circumstances in the Brisbane household," he said, "I think it is best that you stay away. The fact that you are leaving at all makes me wonder . . . have you forgotten about this?" Edmund held up a sheet of foolscap, and the extravagant hand was immediately recognizable as her mother's.

Oh, yes. The list.

Shortly after Edmund had arrived the afternoon before, Mama had presented both him and Selina with a copy of what she called *The Ellis Christmastide List.* On it was row after row of activities she had planned for the next three weeks with dates and times, including the one Edmund's finger hovered next to as he presented the paper to Selina.

"Surely you have not forgotten that we are due in the drawing room in half an hour," Edmund said.

Selina hadn't taken many of the items on the list seriously, half-hoping her mother wouldn't mind her absence. She glanced at the scheduled activity for that afternoon with a grimace.

Return to the Frost Fair in the company of Mrs. Perry and Miss Perry.

Edmund raised his eyebrows, awaiting her reply.

Selina couldn't help but hold Edmund responsible for this list's existence. Mama had never done it before, but she was suddenly eager to be organized and to keep the household busy during the holidays—if only to impress Edmund and outdo Mrs. Perry. Mama had spent the previous afternoon calling on her neighbors to tell them how fascinating the fair had been. Selina should have known Mama would wish to take Mrs. Perry on the ice to show her all that she had been *second* to experience.

Containing her exasperated sigh, Selina slid away from the door and walked several paces away from Edmund. "How could I forget the list?" Her voice was sharper than she intended, but she couldn't help but feel vexed. Noah would be wondering where she was. With Edmund here, would she have to explain her absence more than once? Frustration burned behind her skin, growing hotter as she caught a hint of a smile on Edmund's lips as he adjusted his cravat.

"Do take care to watch your feet this time," he said in a low voice. "If you were to fall on top of me again, people may begin to wonder if it is intentional."

Selina's jaw nearly unhinged as she watched Edmund walk away as if he hadn't just said anything improper—as if he were an entirely innocent, noble gentleman who would never operate under any guise. He stopped by the banister and motioned her forward with a polite smile, his blue eyes clear and bright . . . and far more watchful than she would have liked.

If she was to be forced into going to the Frost Fair with the Perrys, she would have to fetch a different bonnet, one better equipped to protect her from the wind. Grumbling under her breath, she mounted the first four stairs, turning to face Edmund on the fifth. She had once been quite skilled at holding her tongue, especially around Edmund when they had been much younger, but now that he seemed to have forgotten that skill himself, she couldn't stop her words from escaping. "Why are you so eager to accommodate my mother's list?"

"Not to do so would be quite impertinent. I am her guest,

and she has offered me a great deal of hospitality." Edmund's posture straightened. "I would never disobey the wishes of someone who has treated me with such kindness and generosity. Mrs. Ellis has always seemed like a mother to me. For that reason alone, I would obey her wishes."

Selina felt every word as they stabbed into her chest. Edmund had known they would if his unyielding stare was any indication. Did he still believe her desire to marry Noah was based solely on a desire to disobey her mother? How could he not see that she was in love with Noah? She wrung her fingers together, giving Edmund a brief nod. "I too should hate to be discourteous." She lifted her chin, lowering her voice. "After all, soon enough I will be married and visiting this home as a guest; if I wish to be welcomed here as Mrs. Skinner, then I ought to conduct myself kindly over the holidays." Selina gave a warm smile in exchange for Edmund's frown before turning on her heel. She marched up the stairs to her bedchamber, closing the door behind her.

Having Edmund here would be more difficult than she had thought. Perhaps she could communicate with Noah through letters instead. There had to be other ways to meet him without Edmund discovering them. She had always had a quick imagination and a knack for creativity. Surely she would find a way.

Taking a deep breath, she replaced her bonnet and straightened her pelisse, then pulled her gloves up higher on her wrists. With Edmund and Mrs. Perry and her unattached daughter in attendance, the fair was sure to be even more interesting than the last time.

❄

"I have often pondered on the methods of dying I would least prefer." Miss Ruth Perry's soft voice floated up to Edmund's ear. She clung tightly to his arm as her feet moved slowly over the ice. Her expression was smooth and contemplative, not betraying a hint of fear—only deep thought. "I have decided that I would much rather freeze to death than burn. The effect of the cold ice on the skin would soon numb the senses." She glanced at him with wide brown eyes, two locks of auburn hair escaping her hat. "Would you agree?"

"I must admit I haven't given much thought to the topic, but I suppose you are right." Edmund smiled. Though Miss Perry was certainly an interesting walking companion, Edmund kept his eyes fixed on Selina, who walked just a few paces ahead of them. He didn't expect Mr. Skinner to be at the fair again, but Selina was known for her attempts at sneaking away.

Though it was on Mrs. Ellis's list, Edmund hadn't been fond of the idea of coming to a place as public as the Frost Fair. If Mr. Skinner knew that Edmund was staying with the Ellises—his grandmother's will would be turned to ash, and Selina would make the worst mistake of her life. It would help matters if Selina was a little less stubborn.

Edmund tried to take a calming breath, but the frigid air was heavy in his lungs.

Just ahead of Selina, Mrs. Ellis stood with her arm linked through Mrs. Perry's, though she was far more concerned with Edmund and Miss Perry than she was with her own companion. Mrs. Ellis's eyes flitted to her daughter behind her.

"My dear Selina, why don't you take Sir Edmund's other arm? I fear you will slip and fall again." She turned to Mrs. Perry.

"Oh, you should have seen how gallant Sir Edmund was that day. He saved *my daughter* from a terrible accident on the ice."

Selina glanced in Edmund's direction, her mother's sharp eye still fixed on her. "Go on, my dear. I shall not rest until I know you are in such capable hands again. We are walking on the River Thames, for heaven's sake. One cannot be too careful." She let out a shrill laugh for Mrs. Perry before giving Selina yet another pointed look.

Selina finally obeyed, stopping to take Edmund's right arm. Miss Perry leaned around Edmund with a smile. "Oh, Miss Ellis, you are so fortunate to have come to the Frost Fair twice. I fear I will be unable to experience all it has to offer in one afternoon."

Selina smiled, but a hint of frustration still showed in her eyes. "Indeed, it is quite spectacular."

Edmund watched the lines in her brow return as she faced forward once again, where Miss Perry couldn't see her. She likely didn't know Edmund was watching, otherwise, she wouldn't have let her emotions show on her face. She didn't appear angry or frustrated anymore, but rather concerned. Was she worried about what Skinner would think of her absence? It would do him good to worry over the security of Selina's money coming into his possession. The reminder of Edmund's conversation with Skinner made his vision blot dark with anger. How could he so spitefully use a young woman like Selina? Every childhood memory Edmund had of Selina testified of a heart that would one day be easily stolen—easily deceived.

When she caught him watching her, she shot a scowl in his direction before fixing her gaze forward. He hadn't been as discreet as he had planned with his attempts to foil her tête-a-tête this afternoon. Surely she suspected his scheme, and he couldn't blame her for casting him such a fierce glare. If only he could *tell her* why he was being so protective, she might realize he didn't deserve it. She might even thank him.

"Mama!" Miss Perry excused herself from Edmund's side before walking forward to grasp her mother's arm. She pointed at the fire far ahead—at the sheep slowly turning on a spit over the open flame. It wouldn't surprise Edmund if she were asking her mother the same peculiar question she had asked him about her preference for burning or freezing to death. At the moment, Edmund would take either over the deadly daggers Selina was throwing with her gaze.

Edmund cleared his throat, ignoring the look of victory on Mrs. Ellis's face now that Miss Perry was no longer on Edmund's arm. He glanced down at Selina. Her cheeks and lips were pink, her blonde curls soft on her brow. He never would have imagined such a pretty face to be capable of such a dastardly glare.

"I cannot help but feel that you are upset with me." Edmund barely withheld a teasing tone from his voice.

Selina's frown persisted. "What has given you that indication?"

"Your reluctance to take my arm, your silence on the drive here, and the way you continue staring at me as if you wish that I was that sheep." He nodded toward the fire burning hot beneath the roasted animal.

Her lips pinched together as she fought a smile—likely brought on by the accuracy of his words.

"I take it you were quite disappointed to not be visiting Miss Brisbane," Edmund said.

41

Selina's blue eyes met his, a crease still between them. "You know I was not visiting Miss Brisbane. If it was Miss Brisbane I was visiting, you would not have stopped me." She faced forward once again.

Edmund bit his lower lip. If he made an enemy of Selina already, she would be even more eager to sneak away with Skinner. There was a fine balance he needed to find between being her friend and still keeping her away from Skinner. He had been failing at the former already. "You know," he said, "everything is worth far more at the Frost Fair."

"So I have heard."

Edmund followed her gaze to where an elderly woman walked away from a booth wearing a new pair of gloves, a tag hanging off the side displaying the lofty price.

"So . . . you might be keen to accept my apology here, where it's worth at least thrice its value."

Her eyes flitted up to his.

"I am sorry for interfering in your affairs more than I ought to." He held his breath. He nearly told her he wouldn't do it again, but he wasn't a liar. Skinner, however, was one, and that was why he refused to make any undue promises.

Selina studied his face for a long moment. "I'm afraid I cannot afford such an expensive apology."

"I offer it at no cost."

"With you, there always seems to be a cost." She eyed him carefully. "Perhaps you are using this apology as a means of buying my trust? Encouraging me to turn a blind eye to your schemes against Mr. Skinner and me?" Her voice was barely audible as they approached the other three women who had stopped at the end of a line to purchase tea.

Edmund clamped his mouth shut. Selina was more observant than he had given her credit for.

Before they could finish their conversation, Mrs. Perry turned to face him, a bright smile on her cheeks. She had auburn hair much like her daughter, with eyes just as round, and a similarly petite stature. Aside from at least twenty years of age, Mrs. Perry's meddlesome smile and the competitive spark in her eye were the things that differentiated her most from her daughter and related her most to Mrs. Ellis.

"Sir Edmund, are you fond of music?"

Edmund pulled his attention away from Selina, blinking to focus more clearly on Mrs. Perry's cheerful face. "Indeed, I am."

"Then you might be delighted to know that my daughter is a very accomplished singer. She was asked to perform in the home of the Duchess of Rye."

Miss Perry beamed at the praise.

"Is that so, Miss Perry? I may have to press you for a performance before I leave London." Edmund smiled politely. Mrs. Perry's chin lifted in Mrs. Ellis's direction.

"*If* Sir Edmund has time to hear such a performance," Mrs. Ellis blurted with a stiff smile. "He is our guest for several weeks and we have many activities to fit into such a short time."

"You mustn't bring such a charming man into the neighborhood and expect to hide him away." Mrs. Perry chuckled. "Oh, no, you must allow us all to share in Sir Edmund's company." Her gaze slid to her daughter.

Mrs. Ellis's face darkened a shade, her eyes narrowing slightly as she seemed to gather her composure. Edmund glanced down at Selina, who seemed prepared to act as second to a duel at any moment.

"Well, Sir Edmund is so amiable and such a dear and lifelong friend of *my family* that I doubt he would ever object to distributing his company equally among all those of my acquaintance who might desire it." Mrs. Ellis's voice picked up speed. "As he is spending Christmas with us this year, his company will primarily be enjoyed by my daughter, as she and Sir Edmund have been acquainted since childhood. If you would like, you may join us for our Christmas day feast where my cook's famous plum pudding will be served." She paused, taking a breath. "The *Duke* of Rye once came to dine at our house and inquired after my cook's particularly unique method."

Selina's brow furrowed as she watched her mother, her gaze darting up to Edmund and back again.

"I have never seen a woman so proud of plum pudding," Edmund whispered for just Selina to hear.

She exhaled sharply. "She has never been so proud before."

"I take it the Duke has never dined at your house?"

"Never." Selina glanced up, a look of bewilderment widening her eyes.

Edmund suppressed his smile, catching sight of a faint one on Selina's lips. If she could manage to share in his amusement, then perhaps she didn't hate him as much as he thought. His apology might have been accepted after all. He watched the side of her face, his gaze settling on the dimple in her round cheek that flickered in and out as she fought against her smile. As a boy, he had teased her about that dimple, but now it occurred to him that he might have found it just as lovely then as he did now.

Her eyes met his again before leaping away. She looked down at her boots as her mother and Mrs. Perry fought, in a roundabout way, over whose daughter would capture Edmund's attention. Edmund swallowed against his dry throat, turning to face the quarreling women, driving the image of Selina's smile from his mind.

If he wasn't careful, that fight would end in Mrs. Ellis's swift victory.

CHAPTER 6

❄

How many miles can Mrs. Perry really walk on the ice? The woman had insisted they stay at the fair much longer than Selina had anticipated, attempting to visit almost every booth and attraction the fair had to offer. By the time the group finally made their way back to the coach, Selina was in great danger of her plan not working. If Mrs. Perry hadn't worn herself out at the fair, then she surely would have been successful.

What harm would it do to ask?

Selina stopped outside the first coach, the one she had taken with Edmund and Mama on the way to the fair.

"Miss Perry," Selina said, tipping her head to one side. "The green ribbon you were admiring . . . the costly one . . . I believe I saw one almost identical to it at the shop on Oxford Street. Shall we all make a stop there before returning home?" She waited, holding the sides of her coat to keep her fingers from their nervous fidgeting. The solicitor's office was near enough that

Selina could sneak away to see Noah while the others were distracted by the ribbons. She avoided Edmund's gaze as it bore into the side of her face.

Miss Perry turned to her mother with a broad smile. "And the ribbon at the shop is likely to be at least half the price! May we go, Mama? You might even find something to eat in town since the lines were too long at the fair."

"I am quite starved." Mrs. Perry smiled at her daughter. "Very well. Let us find this green ribbon. Will you all be joining us?"

Selina could see her mother's exhaustion as clearly as Mrs. Perry's, the fatigue of both likely brought on by their attempts to outdo one another more so than the walking. But with Mrs. Perry's question pointed at Edmund, Mama could have no choice but to accept rather than leave Edmund alone with the Perrys. Selina would have to find a way to make it clear to her mother that she was not interested in marrying Edmund before her hopes became too high. Though Selina feared it was too late for that. Her mother had likely only invited Edmund to stay at all for that very purpose.

Well, Mama would have to be disappointed. Selina would never think of Edmund in that way, no matter how handsome he was. One could be both handsome and irksome, and the latter would always prevail.

"We would be delighted to join you," Mama said. "If Sir Edmund agrees."

Edmund nodded with a smile, though Selina doubted he was really so enthusiastic about going shopping in the cold. It was rumored that the streets were covered in nearly as thick a layer of ice as the river.

"We will meet you at the modiste's," Mama said, turning to take Edmund's hand as she entered the coach. Selina rested her hand lightly on his as she stepped inside, catching his gaze briefly. She had never seen a pair of eyes quite so penetrating. There was no question he had guessed her reasoning for wanting to make one more stop. But since he had apologized, she could only hope that he would leave his meddling behind long enough for her to escape to the solicitor's office.

After several minutes of listening to Mama speak about her Christmastide plans and Selina keeping her legs as stiff as possible to avoid her knees bumping against Edmund's, they reached their destination. Fresh snow had begun falling, spiraling down in fat flakes onto the icy street.

Inside the modiste shop, Selina led Miss Perry to the spool she had noticed the week before. Fortunately, it was still there, a thick velvet that Selina assured Miss Perry would look striking with her hair.

"I can think of no color that would complement your features better," Selina said. "Do you agree, Sir Edmund?" She glanced up at him from his place beside her—the place he had failed to leave for the last ten minutes.

He nodded, smiling down at Miss Perry. "And surely the price seems quite reasonable after what you saw at the fair."

"Indeed! How could it not?"

As Miss Perry continued speaking with Edmund, Selina backed away a few steps, eyeing the door, then Mama and Mrs. Perry, who stood near the ribbons as well. Both women were distracted enough by the attention Edmund was paying Miss Perry to allow Selina to sneak out.

Thankfully there wasn't a bell to betray her exit, so she

hurried down the street as fast as the ice and snow would allow, wrapping her coat more tightly around herself. She had only a few short minutes to speak with Noah. If she could catch his attention from his window in his office, he might come out to meet her so she could explain why she hadn't come for their usual visit.

When she reached the front doors, she looked up to the office window. With his father out of town, he had often been occupying the front office. The desk was partially visible through the open drapes, as well as part of his chair. She squinted, catching sight of his shoulder and hair as he sat forward, leaning his head on one hand. Was he upset? Had she done that to him? Her heart stung at the thought. She moved closer, debating over whether or not she should make a loud noise to call his attention.

"Selina! Where on earth are you going?"

Mama.

Selina turned away from the window, searching for an explanation for why she had stopped in front of the solicitor's office. Mama held each side of her bonnet to block out the snow, peering out from under it with a frown. Standing just a few paces behind her was Edmund.

He must have seen her leave and known exactly where she would be going.

Selina's jaw tightened as she met his gaze and the false innocence on his face. Hadn't he just told her he was through with his meddling? Despite the cold, her skin grew hot.

"Isn't this the way to the bakery?" Selina asked in an innocent voice.

"No." Mama appeared affronted that Selina could have

forgotten a detail like that. "Are you feeling unwell?" Her expression shifted to concern as she approached, wrapping her arm around Selina's shoulders.

"A little," Selina said. Feeling unwell could easily excuse her strange behavior. They had been out in the cold all afternoon, so it wasn't implausible to claim faintness.

As they passed Edmund, Selina shot him a glare. He looked down at his boots, crossing his arms over his chest.

"Oh, there you are!" Mrs. Perry walked up the street behind Edmund, her daughter in tow. "We have purchased the ribbon. With the snow, I daresay we are better off returning home promptly."

"Oh, yes, to be sure," Mama said, leading Selina down the street toward the coaches. "And not to worry about missing the bakery. My plum pudding is aging beautifully at the moment, so you will have a delicious treat in a few days at our Christmas feast."

"Our stir-up Sunday too was a success," Mrs. Perry said. "I shall bring my pudding as well if you'll allow it."

"That will not be necessary." Mama shook her head fast. "My cook has prepared a very large one this year that will feed us all plenty."

Mrs. Perry pursed her lips. Before she could say another word, Mama turned to Edmund. "Forgive me, but I think I must ride home with Mrs. Perry and Miss Perry. We have many details to discuss about our Christmas feast."

Selina's gaze snapped up to Edmund as he nodded his agreement, looking just as uncomfortable as Selina felt. How could Mama leave her to ride home alone with Edmund? Did she realize how improper that would appear? Yes, he was a close family friend, but Mama hoped for much more than that. Son-in-law to be exact. The disgruntled look on Mrs. Perry's face was all the reward Mama needed as she climbed into the coach with the Perrys.

Before Edmund could comment, Selina walked ahead to their coach, taking his hand as quickly as possible as she mounted the step and sat down on the velvet cushion. She pressed herself as far as possible into the corner, and Edmund settled into the opposite corner, closing the door behind him. As the coach rolled forward, the air inside seemed to grow colder. Silence reigned for a long moment, the crunching of snow and ice under the wheels the only sound. Selina balled her hands inside her gloves, daring a glance at Edmund's face.

She half-expected to find him remorseful, avoiding her eyes as he had been outside. But instead, he gazed out the window with a twist on his lips . . . one that looked suspiciously like a smirk.

When he noticed that she was watching him, he corrected the expression, his eyes rounding slightly in alarm. Perhaps her glare was as intimidating as she hoped.

"Was it you or my mother who first noticed that I left the shop?" She kept her voice even.

"That is difficult to say." Edmund took off his hat, running his gloved fingers through his curls. He glanced up from under his lashes. "Did you think your exit would go unnoticed? Exactly how long did you think you would be able to spend at Skinner's office before your absence at the shop was noted?" The light tone of his voice sent a surge of irritation through her skin. He seemed . . . amused by the entire thing, the glint in his eyes making a mockery of her behavior. Her blood boiled.

"I thought I could see him long enough to tell him why I did not come earlier today. We had agreed to meet at one o'clock and because of your interference, I was unable to go. You claimed to be sorry for your actions earlier, but I cannot believe your apology if you would not let me see him for one moment. *One moment* without alerting my mother."

Edmund shook his head. "I am sorry for how my interference makes you feel, but I am not sorry for interfering."

Selina gritted her teeth. "You promised me your silence."

"My silence, I did promise." He glanced out the window before meeting her gaze again. "But I never promised I wouldn't do all I could to protect you and your reputation. Skinner is not an honorable man."

"What evidence do you have of that? He has shown me far greater respect and goodness than you ever have," Selina snapped.

Edmund gave a hard laugh before shaking his head. "I cannot tell you how I know, but you must listen, just the same. Skinner is not to be trusted."

"I think it is you who I should never have trusted. I would never have invited you to stay at our home if I had known you were plotting a secret way of destroying my engagement."

"Shall I tell your mother today? Would that please you? Whether you like it or not, you have no way of escaping me for the next three weeks unless you want your secret revealed. My honor demands that I continue my efforts to distance you from Noah. His lies will become evident to you eventually, and you will be grateful for my interference."

Selina huffed out a breath. In a moving carriage, alone with Edmund, she couldn't commit his murder without being a suspect, though she dearly wished she could. How dare he treat her like a child? He was not in any position to protect her from who he thought Noah to be. He couldn't claim to know Noah better than she did. Edmund was a hypocrite of the worst sort to act as Noah's superior.

"You cannot prevent me from seeing my betrothed." Selina inched forward on her seat, leaning closer to Edmund so not a single one of her words could be misunderstood. "Our love is strong enough to persist through any of your efforts to destroy it."

He glanced upward with a sigh. "You do not love him."

"Yes, I do."

Edmund leaned forward in his seat, his eyes sharp and unyielding. "No, you do not."

Selina scoffed, anger rising in her chest. "You do not know my heart, Edmund! No one knows it but me." Selina blinked hard, leaning back in her seat. Her breath quickened and she looked out the window. It had taken a great deal of effort to ensure no one knew her heart. She had hidden it away from her family for years. From Mama and from Rose. Being loved second did such things to a heart. It made a heart careful about what it was allowed to feel and who it was allowed to love. Noah was far from what her mother would have chosen for her, just as she was far from what Mama would have chosen for a child. She was not the talented, beautiful Rose, and she was not the heir years of heartache and effort had tried to produce.

She shushed her emotions, turning them back to the anger she had felt just moments before. Edmund leaned his elbows on his knees, looking up at her. "I am sorry, Selina. I am only trying to help you—"

The moment the coach stopped in front of the house, she held up a hand to stop him. "An apology here is worth even less than the false one you gave at the Frost Fair." She met his eyes as he closed them, shaking his head.

Lifting her chin, she exited the coach without assistance, marching toward the front door of the house.

If he had found a way around their bargain, then so would she. All he had asked for was an invitation to stay at the house. As long as he was welcome there, he would stay.

Which meant she only needed to find a way to make him *unwelcome*.

Her mind raced as an idea formed, growing clearer as she entered the house and smelled dinner cooking in the kitchen. There was something else in the kitchen, aging to perfection, that Mama valued above almost all else . . . even above Sir Edmund himself.

Her precious Christmas plum pudding.

CHAPTER 7

❄

*R*olling to his left side for what felt like the hundredth time didn't serve to help Edmund sleep. His mind had been racing all day, and he had been looking forward to when he could go to bed to clear his thoughts and make a plan that would satisfy his worry.

If he didn't stop Selina, she would be deceived and trapped with Skinner for the rest of her life.

If he *stopped* her, Edmund would be without an inheritance.

He rolled to his right side, pressing his face into the pillow. He had considered every possibility, from sneaking into Skinner's office and stealing back the will, to putting Selina on a leash to keep her from sneaking out to see Skinner. As long as he kept his presence in the Ellis home a secret, then how could Skinner really know that Edmund was behind Selina's apparent disinterest?

But she wasn't disinterested at all. She still seemed determined to marry that despicable man, and even more so now that she knew Edmund was wholeheartedly working against it.

He let out a long sigh, staring up at the dark ceiling. He hadn't meant to be so forthright about his intentions to thwart her, but she had been so accusatory in the coach, he hadn't been able to help himself. Now he could think of no possible way the situation would end positively. Selina was doomed. Edmund was doomed. Skinner, it seemed, would be the only winner.

There had to be another way. A new idea had been hovering just out of reach all day, and Edmund hadn't yet grasped it. His frustration rose by the second.

As he struggled to quiet his mind, a rustle sounded outside his door.

The faint shuffle of feet and another rustle. A soft glow of candlelight flickered in the space under Edmund's door, barely noticeable in the darkness.

He sat up, swinging his legs over one side of his bed. The glow wasn't leaving his door, but the rustling had stopped. His time as a soldier may have made him quicker to assume a threat, but so had his conversation with Selina today. She had looked at him as if she had wanted to wring his neck, and it was quite possible that she had come to do it in his sleep. He shook the idea from his mind, nearly laughing at the ridiculousness of it.

Of course not. She would send a servant to do the deed.

Only partially believing his theory, Edmund walked to the door in four long strides. He at least had to confirm whether his suspicions were correct or not. Before the person on the other side of the door could have a chance to move, Edmund pulled it open in one quick sweep.

A sharp gasp came from the woman directly in front of him;

only when the heavy cloth sack she was holding fell to the ground did Edmund notice her face.

Selina.

Her eyes rounded as she covered her mouth, staring down at the floor just outside Edmund's door. The cloth bag, it seemed, had been filled with some sort of dark brown concoction that was now crumbled on the floor. He breathed deeply through his nose, the scent of brandy and fruit wafting up from the mush on the ground.

His gaze jerked up to Selina, who had yet to even venture to explain her presence at his door in the middle of the night. Her hair was tied back loosely, curls spilling out around her shocked expression. She was still dressed as she had been at dinner; she clearly hadn't even tried to go to sleep.

"What have you done?" she blurted in a whisper.

Edmund raised his eyebrows, his confusion doubling. "What have *I* done?"

Selina rubbed one hand over her forehead, stepping back a pace. Her rounded eyes took in his appearance in one quick sweep before she averted her gaze. Edmund had forgotten that he was still dressed for sleep, not at all presentable for a lady. He raked a hand over his hair, moving partially behind the door. "What the devil are you doing outside my room at this hour? I thought you were—" He stopped himself, shaking his head at the mess on the ground. "And what the *devil* is that?" Under any ordinary circumstances Edmund would not have used such words in the presence of a lady, but this was the opposite of ordinary.

"The plum pudding," Selina breathed, setting down her candle and bending down to scoop the mush back into the cloth

57

sack. The moist crumbs and pieces of dried fruit appeared somewhat familiar now, or rather, the remnants of it, the strong scent bringing back memories of Edmund's Christmases with his grandmother.

Selina gave up her effort to retrieve it after just a few seconds, absently wiping her hands on her skirts. She bit her lip, shaking her head in obvious distress. "Mama will have my head," she whispered to herself.

Edmund narrowed his eyes as he recalled the quiet movements he had heard outside his door, the way the flickering candlelight had stopped in front of his room. Considering that she was startled enough to drop the pudding when Edmund opened the door told him that she was not taking a leisurely nighttime turn about the house. She did not want to be caught —and especially not by Edmund.

He crossed his arms, casting her a pointed look. "And I suspect you hoped your mother would have *my* head instead?"

Selina's gaze snapped up to his, unapologetically guilty.

Edmund gasped in disbelief. "You came here intending to destroy the pudding and leave the remnants outside my door. Did you not?"

She didn't deny it, glancing down at the abandoned pudding. One of her shoulders gave a slight shrug, her lips pursing into a small heart before the words burst out. "I would have succeeded if you hadn't given me such a fright."

"*I* gave you a fright? You were the one lurking outside my room in the dark." He leaned against the door which he still held halfway open to conceal his improper attire. "Did you think your mother would send me packing if she thought I destroyed her pudding?" A sudden urge to laugh took over his body, and he rubbed one side of his face as a chuckle escaped him. "How did you plan to explain it? That I became ravenously hungry in the night and stole away to the kitchen for something to eat? That the meticulously wrapped, treasured plum pudding was the best thing I could find?" His laughter intensified. "You planned to frame me as a madman if that is the case."

Selina glared at him, the candlelight intensifying her expression. Her voice was a rasped, fierce whisper, one that surely would have been a shout if not for the late hour. "What other choice did I have? You have no plans to stop meddling in my courtship, so I had to at least try to dispose of you before you destroy everything."

His eyes shot open, his thoughts traveling back to his first suspicions of her presence outside his room. "Dispose of me?"

Selina put one hand against her head, pacing back another step. "I mean . . . have you cast out of the house by my disgruntled mother."

Edmund gave a hard laugh. "And you thought the plum pudding would accomplish that?"

"It would have been the perfect way to start."

"So you had other plans for disposing of me? What are they? You may as well tell me now." He leaned his head farther through the space between the door and the frame. By the way his dark curls itched on his forehead, he could tell his hair was very disheveled. Perhaps it would intimidate Selina the way she attempted to intimidate him with her glaring.

Selina scoffed, planting her plum-pudding-covered hands on her hips. "Until you tell me your plans of *disposing* of my hopes of happiness with Mr. Skinner, then I will do nothing of the sort."

Edmund sighed. "Well, if you are going to continue trying to have me cast out of this house, then our bargain may be in violation."

"How?" Selina snapped, taking a step closer. The fire from her candle lit up the flash of anger in her eyes, and Edmund almost shrunk back. He would have never told her so, but she was surprisingly beautiful when she was angry, even when her rage was directed at him. "You found a way around the agreement we made. Am I not allowed the same? All that was required of me was to secure you an invitation to stay, but I never promised how long it would last. All that was required of you was to keep silent about my courtship, and so you have found other methods of preventing it. All I have done is attempt to match you in your subterfuge, Edmund. Every effort I make to have you sent away will be fair."

Edmund studied her for a long moment. She was quite serious. He took a deep breath. "Your mother would never send me away."

Selina's nostrils flared. "Perhaps she would if you appeared to be forming an attachment to Miss Perry. That would vex her to no end. She would likely be unable to bear even looking at you, especially if you were *also* responsible for her plum pudding being unpresentable. My mother has been known to feign illness to drive unwanted guests away before, and no guest would be more unwanted than you if you were bound in honor to marry the daughter of her longest rival." Selina raised her chin as she caught her breath; she obviously hadn't planned on making that confession, but it was clear her pride had demanded it. "I will continue with my plan, you know. Just as you told me you will still continue with yours. I will not have you fight against me without fighting back."

Edmund closed his eyes, exhaling long and slow. It was worse than he had thought. He wouldn't believe Selina incapable of any level of sabotage, especially not when he appeared to be sabotaging her for no reason. But framing his attachment to Miss Perry was much more serious than a mishap involving plum pudding. His anxiety rose along with his frustration.

They stared at each other for a long moment, neither willing to speak or surrender. Their eyes were locked in a stalemate. In the candlelight, Selina's eyes appeared grey like the bars of a cage. Edmund was trapped.

Couldn't he just let Selina marry Skinner?

She was ungrateful and spiteful and unwilling to be advised. How could he continue trying to help someone who didn't want to be helped, all while facing the potential loss of his inheritance? If his conscience would allow it, he could send Selina away with Skinner in her blissful ignorance and keep his grandmother's will safe from the flames. But behind Selina's fierce eyes, Edmund saw the quiet girl he had known all his life. Submissive, silent, always following in the shadow of her older sister. Edmund had pitied her at times, watching as her sister was showered with gifts and praise while she was ignored.

How could he knowingly send her into a life where she would yet remain in second place? Above all else—money, status, and life itself—a husband should treasure his wife. Selina deserved that, even if she had been plotting to dispose of Edmund. From her perspective, Edmund was behaving in a way deserving of every scheme she plotted against him. He couldn't blame her for her fighting spirit. In fact, he couldn't help but admire her for it. She had grown a great deal from that submissive, quiet girl.

"Unless," Selina finally said, her voice firm. "Unless you would like to strike a new bargain wherein you agree not to stop me from seeing Mr. Skinner, and I agree to stop my schemes as well. We can simply tolerate one another until the frost melts, and you can leave London." She watched him expectantly.

Edmund let out a sigh, rubbing his eyes. Why was he tired now? He had been wide awake moments before when he had been trying to sleep. Perhaps his mind had finally reached its capacity. "Very well." He met her eyes. "You have left me with no other choice."

"Did you truly just agree so quickly? I thought you were too stubborn for that."

"I am by far the least stubborn person in this hallway." He cast her a pointed look.

Selina glanced both ways, her brow furrowing. "I am not stubborn. I am in love. Love is the only thing that could alter my character so much. Love is more powerful than you or me or my mother's ambitions for me."

Edmund wouldn't bother arguing against her claim that she was in love with Skinner. Perhaps she was in love with the idea of him or the attention he gave her, but nothing more. His head ached, and he closed his eyes. The idea he had been struggling to grasp still hovered in his mind, just out of reach. What could he do now?

Footsteps sounded from down the hall, a shuffling gait that was coming too quickly for Selina to move. Her gaze shot up to Edmund, then to the pudding on the floor. Before they could be seen together, he slipped back into his room, shutting the door softly behind him. The last thing he needed was a member of the household spreading rumors about a secret meeting between him and Selina in the night. Mrs. Ellis would force a marriage between them without a moment's hesitation.

At least then Selina would be safe from Skinner.

He leaned one ear against the door, listening as the steps grew closer and stopped. A gasp echoed in the hallway. "Selina, what are you do—" The high-pitched whisper could only have belonged to Mrs. Ellis, and by the way it stopped abruptly, Edmund guessed that she had seen the dismantled plum pudding at Selina's feet.

Good. Selina deserved to be caught for scheming up something so ridiculous. What punishment would Mrs. Ellis concoct for such a dastardly act? He almost smiled as he listened to Mrs. Ellis catch her breath. By the increased volume, he could tell she had moved closer to the door.

"My pudding! You—" Her voice trailed off. "What will Mrs. Perry think? She will think I fabricated the very existence of it! It cannot be recreated in time for Christmas. That is only three days away! The aging will not be proper. The flavor will be wrong." The flustered words continued until her voice took on an edge of anger. "What are you doing out in the hall with my pudding at this hour? Did you mean to sneak it back to your room and taste it? Could you not have waited three days?"

Edmund bit his lip. The ridiculousness of the situation combined with his lethargic, tired state, tempted him to laugh. He held back the sound, leaning his ear back to the door.

"Mama! You cannot do that. Please, Mama, I am sorry. Is there not something else you could take away?"

Edmund's brow furrowed. He had missed the punishment

Mrs. Ellis meant to inflict. By the desperation in Selina's voice, it must have been quite harsh. Selina spoke again, her soft voice shaking with distress.

"Please, Mama," she choked. "It was an accident."

A surge of pity unfolded in Edmund's chest, and he tipped his head back with exasperation. All it took was a quivering of a lady's voice and he was a servant to compassion. Whatever Mrs. Ellis had tried to take away from Selina must have been a far greater penalty than her crime warranted. While he had hoped for her punishment just moments before, he now felt the sting of her soft, cracking voice in his heart. Blast his compassion. It had never served him well. He always ended up trampled on. The stubborn woman would likely not even be grateful.

Taking a deep breath, he pulled open the door enough to lean his head and shoulders through, startling the two women. They turned to face him, and he noticed a sheen of tears in Selina's eyes. She blinked hard, staring at him as if he were a ghost that had just materialized in the hallway. Yes, he'd had every intention of staying hidden in his room, but there was no turning back now.

"Oh! Sir Edmund! My sincerest apologies for having awakened you." Mrs. Ellis's face was a dark shade of crimson—a combination of her anger and embarrassment no doubt.

Edmund shot a quick glance at Selina before clearing his throat. "You did not awaken me, Mrs. Ellis. It must have been I who caused both you and your daughter to come investigating this hallway."

"Pardon me?" Mrs. Ellis's brow scrunched.

With a sigh, Edmund raked a hand over his hair. If he was going to do this, he ought to put on a good act. "I am ashamed to confess that I have a propensity for walking in my sleep. I have done so since I was a child."

She gasped. "You cannot be serious."

"I am, indeed. Considering all the conversation regarding your plum pudding at the fair today, I suppose I developed a strong desire to taste it." He glanced at the mess on the ground, casting his eyes downward in shame before looking up.

Mrs. Ellis's eyebrows rose in shock. "Do you mean to say you . . . you stole away to the kitchen in your sleep to steal my plum pudding?"

He released a long sigh. "I confess, I did. I was entirely unaware of my actions, of course, but I assume, by the taste of fruit and brandy on my lips, that I did indeed take a taste before I awoke, and that it was indeed delicious enough to be recommended by a duke, just as you professed." He gave Mrs. Ellis the most genuine look he could muster. He could feel Selina's shocked gaze on the side of his face.

As he expected, the lines in Mrs. Ellis's face faded, a bashful smile filling their place. "Do you really believe so?"

Edmund gestured at the floor. "I obviously devoured a great deal of it, and with no small amount of zeal considering the mess I made."

A muffled sound came from Selina, and she covered her nose with her knuckles briefly.

Mrs. Ellis didn't appear to notice, her gaze fixed on Edmund. She gave another modest smile. "Oh, my, it seems you did." She laughed, cupping her cheeks between her hands. "Why did you not say so, Selina?" She scowled at her daughter. "I cannot hold this against Sir Edmund if it was so accidental."

Selina continued staring at Edmund, her eyes just as round as before.

"I suppose we shall have to remake the pudding," Mrs. Ellis said, "however it will never age properly in time for Christmas Day. Perhaps we might break tradition a little and serve it on Twelfth Night. I will invite the Perrys to dine with us then instead." Mrs. Ellis's lips curved into a sly grin. "It will have to be prepared and hung to age immediately." She turned to Selina. "You and Sir Edmund should stir it up yourselves. How very festive would that be?" She turned to Edmund expectantly. "Tomorrow morning, if you please."

"It is the very least I can do," he said.

Mrs. Ellis clasped her hands together. "You are so very kind. I suspect with my cook's recipe, and your natural compatibility, you and Selina will make a plum pudding just as delectable as the one you—er"—she gave a stiff smile—"*devoured*."

Natural compatibility? Edmund glanced at Selina from the corner of his eye. Natural enmity was more accurate. She inspired the best and worst in him simultaneously. No matter how striking she appeared in candlelight.

Mrs. Ellis stifled a yawn, wrapping her fingers tightly around Selina's arm. "I will send a maid to clean the floor, and my daughter and I will be off to bed." She paused, casting Edmund a sidelong glance. "And I will see to it that the kitchen remains locked from now on so we may avoid another . . . incident."

Edmund nodded resolutely. "That would be very wise."

Mrs. Ellis bid him goodnight and turned down the hall, the light dimming as they went. Selina glanced back at Edmund just before he closed his door, a look of bewilderment still lingering on her features.

What had compelled him to rescue her? He groaned as he closed the door. Now they would have to make a plum pudding together. It would be a miracle if that didn't end in another fight of some sort. He leaned against the wall, rubbing the back of his neck and closing his eyes. It was over. They had made a new bargain. She had defeated him, and then he had rewarded her by taking the blame for the pudding. He couldn't stop her from marrying Skinner now.

Unless.

His eyes shot open. The idea he had been struggling to grasp all day began to take shape in his mind, making his muscles tense.

Love is more powerful than you or me or my mother's ambitions for me.

Selina had spoken those words, and they now echoed between his ears. She believed she was in love with Skinner, but what if she believed herself to be in love with someone else instead? If Edmund couldn't overthrow her determination to marry Skinner, love—real love—could. What little effort Skinner was making to see Selina, to make her feel treasured, was quite pathetic. He had gotten far with his charms, but combined with a bit of effort, Edmund could do better.

A slow smile pulled on his lips. He was tired. He couldn't have been thinking clearly. But wasn't he already on his way to succeeding? Selina must have been at least a little touched that he would take the blame and save her from whatever punishment her mother had had in store for her. She may have even seen his actions as gallant.

Edmund paced across the room to clear his head. If he could simply show Selina what it meant to be charmed—truly charmed

—by a gentleman, then she might see sense. He wouldn't have to tell her to stay away from Skinner, nor would he have to tell her parents about the courtship. He could keep his end of the bargain. She would want to stay away from Skinner if it meant she could stay by Edmund's side. Then, once her eyes were opened to Skinner's inferior ways, Edmund could return home with his inheritance secured and know that Selina's future didn't include a fortune hunter.

At the moment, there seemed to be no other option.

If Edmund could help it, Selina would be in love with *him* by Twelfth Night.

CHAPTER 8

❄

Edmund Sharp could do no wrong. Selina shook her head at her reflection as she pulled an extra curl out from her coiffure to frame her face. He was much like Rose in that way. An angel in Mama's eyes.

Perhaps even one in reality.

Even after a night of contemplation, Selina couldn't understand why he would take the blame for the pudding. What could his motive have possibly been? She had threatened him with sabotage and yet he had returned the gesture with kindness. Perhaps that was all it was. A kindness. A show of surrender. It had come entirely unexpected, and the image of the soft smile he had left her with as she walked away refused to leave her thoughts. Had he been genuine?

After straightening the long sleeves of her white morning dress, she made her way down to the kitchen where her mother had arranged for her and Edmund to meet. The cook had been just as unhappy as Mama to hear about the pudding incident and had insisted that she be allowed to measure the ingredients prior to Selina and Edmund's preparation of the pudding, just to ensure it was done correctly.

As curious as Selina was to question Edmund, she didn't try to find a way out of the meeting. Learning to make plum pudding sounded like an interesting way to spend the morning, even if it *was* in the company of Edmund. She cringed at the thought of the night before. Her embarrassment was rivaled only by what she felt when she had fallen on him at the Frost Fair. Her cheeks burned with shame. How could she have been so terrible to him? As vexing as he was, he didn't mean to be her enemy. That much was clear by the way he saved her from her mother's wrath. Then what did he mean to be? Her protector? Her jaw tightened. If only he could realize that there was nothing to protect her from.

She started down the hall toward the kitchen. Edmund stood just outside the door. He wore a pale green waistcoat, his dark curls styled neatly, contrary to the night before when they had been spilling over his forehead. She had almost preferred him that way. It gave him a debonair, dangerous look. Her heart fluttered a little at the smile he gave her as she approached. Good heavens, what was wrong with her today? She hadn't slept much, but that had never given her such strange thoughts before.

"Good morning, Selina." Edmund gave a polite bow of his head, his sharp blue eyes taking in her appearance. His gaze settled on her face, roaming her features intensely as he took a step forward. She stared at him, puzzled.

"You look well."

She swallowed, looking down at her hands.

"Especially for someone who spent half the night awake plotting sabotage."

Glancing up, she was surprised to see a broad smile on Edmund's lips.

"It was more invigorating than exhausting," she said.

"Ah. That must account for the brightness of your eyes today." His gaze seemed to search her soul as he continued smiling down at her.

"My eyes are not any *brighter* than they were yesterday." Selina backed up a step, taking a deep breath. "But if you insist there is a difference, it might be because for the first time since you arrived I am not tempted to injure you."

Edmund's eyebrows shot up and a laugh escaped him. "Yes, your glare is absent for once. Perhaps that is why." He still looked at her in that strange way, and she had to look down.

How could she find the humility to apologize? She wanted to ask why he had taken the blame, but she didn't know how. "I—I believe I ought to thank you for what you did last night." She glanced up, a smile pulling on her lips as she recalled how he had explained it. "It must have come at great expense to your pride admitting that you—you . . . "

"Devoured the plum pudding in my sleep?"

Selina laughed, covering her lips with two fingers. "Yes. That." Her giggling continued for several seconds before she could rein it in. Edmund's deep chuckle joined hers, making it difficult to stop. When her laughter subsided, she cast him a curious look. "Why did you do it? I do not deserve your kindness. I especially didn't in that moment."

Edmund dropped his gaze. "From inside my room, it

sounded as though your mother planned to punish you. I knew if I took the blame, neither of us would be punished."

Selina's guilt over her behavior toward him increased. She wrung her hands together. "I was surprised that you weren't *pleased* with my punishment."

"Why would I have been pleased?" Edmund asked, his brow furrowing.

"Because my mother threatened to restrict me from leaving the house for an entire month. No parties, no balls, no trips to any shops or fairs. Essentially, your aim to keep me from Mr. Skinner would have been accomplished." Selina stared up at him with wide eyes. That had been the most curious part of it. Edmund could have claimed his victory, but he had chosen to help her instead.

He blinked down at her, his smile gone. He seemed to be struggling to find words. He cleared his throat. "Well, er—I—decided that you did not deserve such a great penalty for a harmless pudding mishap." He exhaled loudly, offering a fresh smile, but it seemed more forced. "So now you are free to leave the house without opposition, even if you know there isn't a single soul in this household who would be pleased to hear where you are going."

Selina held his gaze for a long moment before releasing a sigh. "Why must you attempt to make me feel so guilty about it?"

"You are guilty of nothing but following your heart." Edmund's expression softened. "Your heart will often pull you where it wants, and it takes great courage not to pull against it. In the tug of war with love, it's easier for us to never pull at all. We are bound to lose, so there is no point exhausting ourselves."

Selina stared at this new and peculiar Edmund. Was he in his right mind? She had never imagined such heartfelt words coming from his lips. She followed after him as he opened the kitchen door. "I thought you said you believed that I didn't truly love Mr. Skinner."

As she passed through the door, Edmund cocked one eyebrow. "Does it matter what I believe?"

Selina paused in front of him, crossing her arms, though her confidence wavered. "No."

"That is what I thought." Edmund smiled down at her before stepping away from the door and starting toward the table where Cook had placed the ingredients and instructions for the plum pudding.

Selina watched Edmund's back as he walked, her confusion rising with each step. When had he ever been so quick to surrender? She followed him, turning her attention to the tabletop. Every ingredient was separated into dishes surrounding a pot at the center of the table. On the opposite side of the room, Cook gave them a cold greeting from the stove, likely still upset over the fact that her pudding had to be remade at all. Her ginger hair hung straight around her face, her narrow shoulders curving in a permanent arch toward the pots and pans she spent so many hours hunched over throughout the day.

Mama had obviously hoped this time Selina would be spending with Edmund would help them grow closer. There was no questioning Mama's intentions in forcing them to make a new pudding. By Cook's watchful eye, it was clear she would have rather made a new one herself.

Selina examined the ingredients: suet, currants, dried fruit, eggs, flour, milk, spices, and brandy. She had little experience with baking but learning something new was always thrilling. If Edmund hadn't been standing so near, she might have smiled or squealed with excitement. But the way she felt his stare on the side of her face made her vastly uncomfortable.

"Have you ever made plum pudding before?" he asked.

"My family has done little more than each taking a turn to stir the pot on stir-up Sunday." Selina smiled. "I confess I am rather ignorant when it comes to cooking."

"With a cook as accomplished as yours, I see no reason for you to learn." Edmund glanced up as Cook smiled their way. He turned toward Selina. "I am certain you will always be in a position to employ a cook."

She looked down at the bowl in front of them. A life with Mr. Skinner could not guarantee an income sufficient to employ a cook, and she had no money of her own. Was Edmund still hinting that she would not marry Mr. Skinner? Her defenses rose. Cuffing the ends of her sleeves, she squared her shoulders. She would have to learn, then.

"I hope you will too." She picked up the instructions, looking them over in one sweep.

"Did you just offer me a positive wish for my future?" He raised his eyebrows in shock. "It seems you are finally coming to like me."

"I did not say that I liked you. I simply . . . owed you a kindness for what you did yesterday."

"Well, I would not call that a fair exchange. You will have to humiliate yourself to spare me a punishment if you want to repay me."

"If your actions were truly out of kindness, you wouldn't require payment."

He chuckled. "It is by no means required, but I might still request it."

She eyed him with misgiving. "What would you request?"

He tapped his chin, his eyes sparking with deep thought. "I would request that you withhold your objections to spending the afternoon in my company. If I am to be here until the roads are safe to travel, we ought to become better acquainted. I don't believe your mother's list has anything scheduled until dinner. Would you grant me that one small request?" He gave a cajoling smile, one that sent a jolt through her stomach. What a strange request. Her heart pounded. Why did Edmund suddenly wish to spend time with her? By the way he was looking at her, a concern took root in her chest. Did he . . .

She shook away the worry. She must have been imagining the admiration in his gaze. At least she hoped she was. It would not do if he developed an attachment to her. He would only end up hurt. A tiny thrill shot through her veins, born from a much younger version of herself who would have been flattered by Edmund's attention. The younger Selina would have been shocked by his smiles and his new habit of speaking more than a few short words at a time. It made him more handsome.

Stop.

She steered her thoughts in a more proper direction.

"Well?" Edmund cast a smile at her dazed expression.

Oh, yes. He had asked her a question. That afternoon she had planned to see Noah. Realization crashed over her shoulders. Of course. That was Edmund's reasoning for wanting to spend time with her. He was still being sneaky. Her brow furrowed into a scowl. "I am otherwise engaged this afternoon." She glanced at the instructions again, avoiding his gaze.

"Very well." Edmund's voice held a note of disappointment that sent another flutter through her stomach. "At least I will see you at dinner."

Selina searched for a way to lighten the air between them. "*If* we finish the plum pudding properly. I am fairly certain my mother would deprive us of the meal if we don't succeed this morning."

Edmund's lips quirked slightly upward. "Well, if she does deprive us, we could simply come back to the kitchen and eat the insufficient pudding ourselves."

Selina gave a quiet laugh as she poured the first half of the milk into the bowl as the instructions noted. "I believe the word you meant to use was *devour*."

Edmund's laugh echoed in the kitchen, deep and hearty. "Forgive me. What a horrific mistake. That is precisely what I meant to say."

She looked up at him, smiling without reservation. When his eyes met hers, she looked down, clearing her throat. "Well, are you going to help me? You are the reason this happened in the first place."

His eyebrows shot up, but he didn't say anything more, a slight smile still lingering on his lips. As he read over the instructions, she studied the side of his face. When had he developed that dimple? It wasn't deep, but it was noticeable, just to the right of his mouth, closer to his chin.

"I must confess . . . I have never cracked an egg with the intent of baking. Keeping out the shells will be a challenge." He picked up an egg and turned it over in his palm.

Cook huffed out a breath in the corner. Mama had likely

instructed her not to interfere, but the struggle she was experiencing not to was evident.

Selina picked up an egg from the row of eight. "With the intent of baking? So you have cracked an egg with another intent?"

A slow smile spread over his cheeks. "The chickens at my family's estate were quite prosperous. As children, my older brother and I would often throw eggs at one another. To our parents' dismay, of course. We even invited other boys from the neighborhood to play. We called the game 'Spill the Yolk.'"

Selina could remember well the first time she met Edmund. He had been just a child, visiting his grandmother in London. His hair had been even more curly then, but not quite as dark. With the serious, shy expression he wore back then, she never would have imagined he was one to throw eggs for amusement.

She eyed the egg in his hand suspiciously. "Surely you don't intend to play another game of 'Spill the Yolk' today? I don't think I would enjoy that game."

Edmund chuckled, taking a step closer. "Are you quite certain?" His smile took on an edge of mischief.

She backed away, laughing, though she knew he wouldn't actually throw the egg at her. "Yes. Now put that down or crack it into the bowl. We have taken far too long already."

He walked closer with that grin, and when she backed away, her back clattered against the table. She whirled around to steady the table, but the remaining eggs were rolling in the opposite direction. She caught the jar of suet before it could tip, and Edmund lunged for the eggs, stopping all but two from falling to the ground.

"Oh, dear." Edmund steadied the eggs on the table and

glanced underneath it to see the two that had fallen and spilled their contents on the floor. With his arms outstretched on the table, he was closer to Selina's height. His face was flushed as he straightened his posture. "Perhaps we can make it with six eggs rather than eight? Would it even make a difference?"

They both glanced up as a withered hand lowered two new eggs forcefully to the tabletop. Cook crossed her arms. "Yes. The texture'll be all wrong. The raisins're already unable to soak in brandy for the proper time." Her eyes darted to Edmund, narrowing slightly. "Take care to follow the instructions without error." She turned around, returning to her cooking across the room, muttering something unintelligible under her breath.

"I feel much like a boy who was just scolded by his mother," Edmund whispered, casting a wary glance at Cook's back.

Selina pressed her lips together to keep from laughing again. "It seems Cook is the only person in London who does not like you."

Edmund rolled up his sleeves, picking up an egg. He tapped it twice against the tabletop before prying it open. A few fragments of the shell escaped into the bowl, and he picked them out. "Is that so?"

Selina nodded, picking up an egg to add to the bowl. She followed Edmund's pattern, cringing as the contents coated her fingers. "Yes. My mother is quite fixated on you, Mrs. Perry and Miss Perry as well, and—"

"And you?"

Selina's gaze shot up to him, protest already rising in her throat. "No. That is not what I was about to say."

Edmund cracked another egg, more successfully this time. He smiled down at the bowl. "You did say that your cook is the *only* person in London who doesn't like me, so from that, I must conclude that you are just as fixated on me as your mother and neighbors are."

Selina scoffed. "There is a difference between liking someone and being fixated on someone."

"Do explain." Edmund cocked his head. He was enjoying her discomfort far too much.

She shifted on her feet as she picked up another egg. "Liking implies a general fondness for one's company." She shook her head fast, discarding her eggshells. "No, not even a fondness. A *tolerance* for one's company. It is neither extremely pleasurable nor extremely miserable to be in the company of someone you simply like."

"I see." Edmund paused his egg cracking. "I am glad to know you are not miserable in my company."

"Not today, though I have been in the past." She gave a slight smile before continuing, "On the contrary, fixation is rather like a deep interest in someone, or treating one with an excessive, unfounded admiration. Fretting about someone day and night, counting their virtues, and yearning to be just as admirable as they are someday."

Edmund's expression had turned serious. His eyes flickered to hers. "Fixation can often be mistaken for something else as well." He paused. "Love."

Selina struck the last egg too hard against the table, catching the spilling yolk between her fingers and thrusting it into the bowl. "Yes, I suspect it could be. The two are similar enough."

"I would have to disagree. They are very different." Edmund met her gaze.

Selina looked away, searching for a lighter subject. She

glanced down at her hands. "Surely my mother still meant this to be my punishment." She shook her fingers above the bowl with a grimace, letting the translucent substance drip off. She laughed at Edmund's grimace as he did the same before pulling out his handkerchief instead. After wiping the tips of his fingers, he took Selina's hand, pulling it toward him.

His eyes met hers before flickering away, and his throat bobbed with a swallow. With methodical movements, he wiped the egg off her hands, starting with her fingertips. She couldn't move as his fingers gently handled hers. A slight shiver trailed up her wrist, and her shoulder tensed. Her first thought was to call the service a kindness, but it wasn't kind at all to make her stomach flutter in such an unnatural way.

If it wasn't for what he had done the night before, she would be locked away in the house for several weeks. It was natural to have positive feelings toward him now, though she was not accustomed to positive feelings toward Edmund. And especially not an increased pulse in his presence.

When he finished, she tugged her hand away and let it hang at her side. "Thank you." She shook out her fingers, afraid they would no longer function after he had touched them like that. She avoided his gaze, staring into the bowl.

"Well, now that the most difficult part is over," Edmund said, "Shall we finish making this blasted pudding?"

Selina's jaw dropped. "Do not let my mother hear you call it that, or she will send you packing for certain."

Edmund laughed, and she caught herself staring at that *blasted* dimple again. When his laughter subsided, he regarded her seriously. "Since you denied my first request, may I ask for something different?"

Selina nodded.

"As you know, I have promised to keep your secret. But when you see Mr. Skinner, please don't tell him you have seen me recently. Please do not mention my name or tell him I am a guest here. Will you keep that one secret for me?"

Selina frowned. She hadn't expected that request. She wanted to ask why, but nodded instead, quietly turning back toward the instruction sheet. "Very well. You have my silence."

He smiled. "Thank you."

Her breath felt suddenly heavy coming in and out of her lungs, made weak and compressed by the sight of that smile. Seeing Noah that afternoon would sort out all these strange feelings, she was sure of it.

CHAPTER 9

Noah stood in the alleyway between his father's office and the neighboring shop. The frigid air tunneled through the alley, biting at Selina's cheeks as she approached him. She had succeeded in getting his attention from the window this time. He smiled as she came closer, and she brought a similar expression to her own face. Edmund had stopped her from seeing him for three days, and by the way Noah took the final two steps to meet her, he seemed to have missed her a great deal. "Selina," he said.

She gazed up at his face as he took her hands in his, running his fingers over her gloved ones. Despite her effort not to, she was reminded of how Edmund had touched her hands that morning. Why had that felt so different? She had been replaying the moment in her mind over and over, unable to identify why it had affected her so greatly. Was it that *all* handsome men caused such feelings within her? She had connected the feeling with the gentleness in Edmund's gaze. Noah was all intensity with his eyes, so that must have been what made the difference. Or the fact that she was wearing gloves this time. That was likely the true reason.

"Selina?"

She glanced up at him with wide eyes. "Yes?"

"I asked where you have been these last three days."

How had she not heard his question? She pushed all thoughts of Edmund out of her mind as quickly as she could, focusing on Noah's worried gaze. His forehead was creased, and the tip of his nose was red from the cold. His dark hair fell over his brow, but it was straight and didn't curl the way Edmund's did.

Good heavens.

She drew a deep breath, bringing a reassuring smile to her lips. "My mother has created a list of all the activities she wishes to have us and our guest participate in for Christmastide. You know how she enjoys controlling everything and everyone within her house." Selina laughed. "It is no matter."

"Guest?" Noah's eyebrows lifted. "Is it not too cold to travel?"

Selina recalled Edmund's request . . . she couldn't tell Noah about him, even if she didn't know why he had asked. Edmund was keeping a much greater secret for her, so she couldn't help but take it seriously. "Oh . . . a female cousin of mine. She arrived before the roads became so treacherous, and now she has been invited to stay at least until Twelfth Night."

"Ah, I see." Noah smiled. "What is her name? I have not heard many tales of your cousins."

Selina bit her lower lip, glancing at the brick wall to her left in search of any sort of inspiration. There was none. "Miss Mildred Ellis." She blurted the first name that came to mind.

"A relative of your father's side, I take it." Noah nodded with understanding. "I wish I was in a position to meet her. If our circumstances were different, I could meet all of your family members." He turned her hands over in his, running his thumb over her palms. "So we must still marry in secret." She waited for the shivers she had felt with Edmund's touch, but she felt nothing. How strange. And frustrating. It had been the longest stretch of time she had gone without feeling vexed by Edmund, but now she was vexed all over again. The reasoning had changed drastically. That was the most unsettling part.

Even more unsettling was the way her stomach flipped at Noah's words, *marry in secret.* Could she really do it? Her legs stiffened and she tightened her jaw. Why was she letting Edmund's words bring any doubts to her mind? What had changed in three days?

"Since we are on the subject . . . " Noah's intense brown eyes met hers. "I have a friend who is willing to convey us to Gretna Green, even in these frigid conditions. The trip will take longer than usual, of course, but I think we should leave sooner than we originally planned."

Her eyes rounded. "How soon?"

"We could depart as soon as the seventh of January."

Selina's heart picked up speed. They had discussed her telling her mother on Twelfth Night, but not eloping the very next day. "I—are you certain the roads will be safe? There is no harm in waiting a little longer. We might even wait until Spring when there will be no risk of ice on the roads." Her words spilled out quickly. She smiled to soften them. "It will simply give us more time to plan."

"When you elope, there is little to plan." He smiled. "And I will take care of all the details to ensure you are warm and comfortable on our journey."

She nodded, though her stomach had begun to twist in knots. *It is completely natural to feel nervous about something so secretive.* "I think we are right to marry in secret. My mother will have to accept my choice to marry you if we are already married. Telling her beforehand would be disastrous." Selina's heart still raced, and it took several deep breaths to slow it down.

"I am very glad you feel that way." Noah gave her hands a squeeze before touching the side of her face. "I thank my good fortune every day to have found a woman like you. I do not deserve you." He cast his eyes downward.

Noah's humility stood in stark contrast to Edmund's earlier teasing when he had implied she was fixated on him. The corners of her mouth lifted, and her nervousness faded a little. Soon she would be out of the cold and back home. Edmund's words flitted through her mind. *At least I will see you at dinner.*

She stopped herself. Why was she so eager to return home? She had been looking forward to seeing Noah since her first visit to the Frost Fair. Her confusion rose again, and she stamped it out. She didn't know how to respond to Noah's words, so she simply glanced down at their interlocked hands, wondering again why it lacked the sensation she had felt earlier that day.

"What does your mother have scheduled on her Christmas-tide list tomorrow?" Noah asked, brushing aside the curls on her brow. "I should like to see you again."

The thought of walking back out in the snow did not sound

appealing when she was already freezing to the bone. "I forgot what she has on the list for tomorrow, but I imagine it will be a busy day after the relaxed schedule for today. Then it will be Christmas Eve, and then Christmas Day. Perhaps on Boxing Day I will see you again?" Her eyes widened. "Or at church on Christmas. Will you be there?"

"I will meet you behind the church when the meeting is over." He smiled. "I look forward to seeing you again. I hope I will have more information to share on our elopement and travel arrangements then."

A heaviness settled in her chest and she swallowed hard, wishing that would be enough to rid her of her discomfort. Now that it was becoming real, her mind raced with doubt. And it was Edmund's fault for planting it there. What if she did have to cook for the rest of her life? What if her mother never forgave her for what she did? Was love really worth all of that? Perhaps fear was stronger than love, and that was why she suddenly felt so heavy with worry.

Noah pulled her into his arms as he had at the Frost Fair before she bid him farewell. Snow swirled heavily in the air, and she hoped, in combination with the hood of her cloak, she would be unrecognizable to any passersby. As she hurried home, her eyes watered. She blamed the cold.

"How is Miss Brisbane faring?" Mama asked as Selina came through the sitting room door. Mama sat on the sofa with an assortment of ribbons on the tea table, examining each red and gold ribbon closely. They would be used to decorate the house on Christmas Eve, and that was Mama's favorite tradition.

"She is well." Selina hoped it was true, but in truth, she hadn't the slightest idea of what sort of health Miss Brisbane was in. Sitting down on the chair closest to the fire, Selina closed her eyes with a sigh, letting the warmth soak into her skin.

"Venturing out in all this cold weather will surely be detrimental to *your* health. Perhaps you should not visit Miss Brisbane so often."

"The Frost Fair is growing more each day, I've heard," Selina said, rubbing her hands together in front of the fire. "It is rumored an elephant was brought into town and walked across the ice."

Mama gasped, dropping the red ribbons she held. "Can it truly withstand such weight? I suppose we had little to worry about. I would not object to going back, although the entrance fees have become quite excessive."

Selina nodded. "Only excessively wealthy people could afford to go back a third time. And, as you have reminded me often, we are not excessively wealthy." She glanced over her shoulder at Mama, who looked down at her lap with a tight-lipped smile. Mama usually looked much more worried when discussions of money came up.

"What is it?"

"Nothing at all." Mama's gaze snapped up before settling on her ribbons again. "I—I was thinking that it would be wise to save the money to purchase new ribbons. These have grown old and out of fashion."

Selina watched Mama with growing suspicion for several seconds before turning back toward the fire.

"I suspect Sir Edmund will be proposing to you before the holidays are through," Mama said.

Selina's heart leaped and she whirled around to face her mother again. She wore a mischievous smile now, running a gold ribbon between her thumb and forefinger. "He does have a way of looking at you that makes me believe he is developing an attachment. He seemed quite pleased to have the opportunity to make a new pudding with you this morning."

Selina was already shaking her head. "No, Mama. It will not do for you to entertain thoughts of Edmund and me . . . being attached in any way."

"Why not?" Mama crossed her arms and slumped against the back of the sofa. "He is handsome and revered and amiable and there is absolutely nothing wrong with him. Nothing at all."

"It seems Mrs. Perry wants him for her daughter," Selina said. "Is that why you arranged for us to make the pudding together this morning? Are you trying to draw us together?"

"Oh, posh! That was my intention long before Miss Perry showed a vexingly obvious interest in him." Mama cast her gaze heavenward before regarding Selina seriously. "You will begin to recognize Edmund's favor for you just as I have. You mustn't do anything to discourage him. We only have him here for a few weeks and you must use them to your advantage. Miss Perry does not have the opportunity to live within the same walls and see him at every meal. I have never been so grateful for frigid weather." Mama giggled. "He cannot leave, even if he wishes to!"

Selina looked down at her fingers. Warmth had finally broken through the numbness. "You are mistaken, Mama. Edmund is quite eager to leave London, and there is nothing that will keep him here when the ice melts. He does not care for me at all. As you said, he is kind to me, and that is what you have mistaken for any attachment you perceived."

Mama pursed her lips. "It is always much easier to perceive an attachment as someone who is not involved in it."

Selina swallowed hard. That was not a comforting notion.

"At dinner tonight, you must observe who his eyes fall on when he first enters the room," Mama said. "I have invited the Perrys and the Folletts. If his eyes fall on you, then I am correct in my assumption that he is attached. If his eyes fall elsewhere, then I will surrender. Edmund is a good man; as such, his gaze will always lean in the direction of his heart. That is how we will know if his fondness for you goes beyond mere familial friendship."

Selina crossed her arms. Was that true? There was so little she knew about such things. Her heart thudded with nervousness as she anticipated the evening. What color could she wear that would ensure Edmund didn't glance her way? The sofa was red. Perhaps if she wore red and sat on the sofa, she would blend into the fabric and be easily concealed. She exhaled sharply, shaking her head. It was ridiculous. One glance could not determine anything. And there was *no reason* Edmund would look to her first, nor was there any reason she would look to him first if she were to walk into a room. In fact, she would likely avoid looking at him in order to *not* experience any more fluttering in her stomach.

The fire was too warm. She stood, turning to face Mama. "You will see that you are wrong. Edmund is not any more interested in me than he is in the furnishings of the drawing room."

"If you are so certain I am wrong," Mama said, lifting her chin, "let us add something to this experiment."

Selina raised her eyebrows.

"If his gaze is drawn to you first, as I suspect, then you must not leave his side tomorrow. The two of you, with my guidance, will spend the entire day in one another's company. You will not leave to make any calls, and you may not shut yourself away in your room."

Selina sighed. "Very well. And if his gaze falls on any other lady in the room, you must encourage him to pay her a visit tomorrow. You must attempt to steer his attentions toward her."

A crease appeared between Mama's brows. "If I must, then I will. That is how confident I am in my success."

Selina took a deep breath. If Edmund did develop an attachment to a different lady, all would be well again. Miss Perry, as well as the Folletts' two daughters, would also be gathered in the drawing room. If he was drawn to one of them and developed an attachment elsewhere, Selina would no longer experience such strange thoughts and feelings toward him, and she would not have to worry that he was growing too fond of her. She loved Noah, and he loved her. That was all. She had told herself that many times.

So why was it becoming so difficult to believe?

CHAPTER 10

The walk to the drawing room felt exceptionally long. Edmund stopped outside the door, listening for a short moment to the voices within. Mrs. Ellis had told him there would be additional guests joining them that night, so that would account for the loud male voices and soft female ones. He had spent most of the day in his room since he and Selina had made their plum pudding. Mrs. Ellis hadn't planned anything for the afternoon, and Selina had declined his request to spend more time with him that day.

Why that had stung so much, he couldn't say. She was not giving up on Skinner yet, so he would have to try a little harder to make her see sense. His efforts to be charming that morning had been rather juvenile, and she hadn't seemed to have been affected by them at all. He had hoped his behavior would at least make her realize that what she felt for Skinner was nothing more than a fixation and that there were other men, like Edmund, who could make her feel even more important.

But she had declined his attention.

He took a deep breath as he thought of the moment he had taken her hands in his. She must have felt something then. How could a sensation like that be one-sided? Her eyes had rounded in shock, but it could have been negative shock, not positive.

He was thinking far too deeply now. He shook out his hands by his sides. Why was he so nervous?

He couldn't let rejections from Selina affect him so greatly any longer. There was no reason to let them strike down his confidence. But he had been dwelling on it all day, thinking of the deceit Skinner was still inflicting on her. She had obviously seen Skinner that afternoon, and there had been nothing Edmund could do to stop it.

When the footman opened the drawing room door, the crowd inside fell silent. Edmund walked through with a lowered gaze before remembering that he should hold his head high. The moment he looked up, his eyes fell on Selina, who was staring at him with wide eyes, slumping back to nearly half her height on the red sofa. The red dress she wore was nearly the exact shade as the cushions . . .

And so were her cheeks.

Her gaze darted away from him instantly, and she looked down at her hands. Mrs. Ellis sat near her daughter, smiling as broadly as he had ever seen her smile, contrary to Selina's expression. Edmund hardly noticed the other guests, focusing once again on Selina's downcast expression. She seemed to be intentionally avoiding his gaze. Was it shyness? He would have considered her aloof if she hadn't been blushing so much. He pressed back the smile that tugged at his mouth. Perhaps his efforts had been successful after all.

After Mrs. Ellis stood and introduced him to the guests, he made his way straight to the left side of the room. There was a space between Selina and the edge of the sofa that he would be a fool not to take. His confidence rose as he strode forward to claim it.

※

No. Selina watched as Edmund started in her direction. *No, no, no.* She could practically feel Mama's pride seeping out of her eyes, shooting straight at Selina to chant over and over that she was right.

Mama might have been right in guessing that Edmund would look at Selina first, but that didn't mean her assumptions about the *meaning* of his look was correct. Of all the people in the room, Selina was the one he knew best. That must have been the only reason he was coming to sit with her.

Selina adjusted her posture. There was no need to try to hide anymore. The red dress hadn't had the effect she had hoped for. Perhaps if she had darker hair like Edmund's, the color could have blended with the dimness of the room. How did he look more handsome than usual tonight? Had he made an extra effort in order to impress her? That would be quite inconsiderate of him. Her stream of anxious thoughts continued, and she distracted herself with her gloves as he came to sit on the cushion beside her.

"Good evening, Miss Selina." His voice was deep and warm, and it sent a jolt through her chest.

"Good evening, Sir Edmund." She shot him a quick glance

from the side of her vision. "I trust you had a pleasant afternoon."

"Not nearly as pleasant as it could have been," his voice lowered slightly, "if you had agreed to spend it with me."

She swallowed against her dry throat. Mama was sitting close enough to hear his words. If he continued in that way, especially if the other guests witnessed it, they would develop the same suspicions as Mama.

In the candlelight, his eyes appeared lighter. Softer. More genuine.

Her heart pounded. "That is not so." She gave a nervous laugh. "If I had agreed to spend it with you, disaster would have surely ensued. You likely had a comfortable, quiet afternoon without any slipping on ice or destroyed puddings or capsized tables." She cast her gaze about the room, focusing on anything but him and his soft, kind eyes.

But she couldn't avoid hearing his voice. "My afternoon was dreadfully boring, actually. I would have much rather been with you."

Perhaps the cold weather was affecting the function of his mind. He would never have been saying these things to her if he were in proper health. When she failed to come up with a response, he spoke again. "Did you have an enjoyable afternoon?"

She glanced up at him. "I visited Miss Brisbane."

Edmund seemed to understand her words immediately, his eyes shifting away from her for what must have been the first time. He tugged at his gloves. "So I assume that means yes, it was enjoyable?"

Selina nodded. "Yes." The moment the word escaped her lips,

her stomach fell. There had been an ill feeling in her heart ever since she had approached Noah that day, and she had been unable to rid herself of it or determine where it had come from.

"You sound uncertain," Edmund said, regarding her seriously. The warmth in his gaze tugged at her heart, and tears burned behind her eyes. He was the only person who knew what she was up to, but he was also the last person to whom she would express her doubts. He would be just like Mama, gloating over how he had been right, and she had been wrong. She would never admit her worries to him; she could sort them out in her own mind well enough. It was his fault they were there anyway.

"Well, it was quite cold outside," Selina said, keeping her voice steady. "That is the only part of the afternoon that wasn't enjoyable."

"I see." Edmund met her gaze. "Have you ever asked Ski—er —Miss Brisbane to come to you?"

"H-she is quite busy with work with her father being out of town."

Edmund's face was unreadable. "If Miss Brisbane cared about your health, she would make the trip regardless." His jaw tightened.

Selina's defenses rose, but they faded as she realized his words held some merit. It *would* be very kind of Noah to come to her instead, but their arrangement had been in place for quite some time. She did not want to do anything that might result in him being seen with her near their house.

"*Miss Brisbane* does care for my health. Please do not worry." Selina spoke with finality, hoping Edmund would drop the subject. She didn't like dwelling on things that fed the worry in her stomach.

A slight smile tugged on Edmund's lips.

"What is it?"

He leaned closer to her ear. "I quite enjoy referring to Skinner as a *Miss*."

Selina scoffed, fighting her own smile. "I will have you know, I referred to you as a *Miss* earlier today."

Edmund's eyebrows lifted. "Pardon me?"

"Yes," she whispered. "You asked that I keep your presence here a secret, and to do that I told Mr. Skinner that my cousin, Miss Mildred Ellis, is the guest at our house."

"Mildred? Could you not have chosen a more fanciful name? One a little more . . . attractive?" He appeared genuinely insulted, and it caused a laugh to burst from her chest. She stifled it instantly when her mother's gaze was drawn to her.

"It was the first name that came to mind."

"Do I look like a *Mildred* to you?"

Selina bit back her laughter again, glancing up at him with a smile. "Now that I have a good look at your face . . . yes, you do."

Edmund scoffed, sitting back. "Well, if I were to give you a *male* name in order to disguise your identity, I would give you a much more attractive name than what you chose for me."

"Oh?" Selina raised one eyebrow. "What would you call me?"

He feigned deep thought before leaning closer with a serious expression. "Edmund."

Selina shook her head. "That name would never suit me. I am not nearly as pompous as the Edmund I know."

His wide smile contrasted sharply with his eyes, which were soft and thoughtful as they roamed her face. "You should be honored. You are the only other person besides myself worthy of such a magnificent name."

Selina knew he meant it as a jest, but his eyes had captured her enough to make laughing impossible. In reality, he *was* humble, and that was why he could say such things without appearing pompous. When she had first seen him at the Frost Fair, she had assumed he was giving himself airs and diminishing those beneath his station, like Noah. But now that she knew him better, she had begun to trust him. His opinion meant more to her now . . . and it was no question that he had a low opinion of her betrothed.

Her heart thudded hard as fear caught up to her again.

She had been wrong. It wasn't Edmund's *words* bringing doubt to her mind. It was his actions that were bringing doubt to her *heart*. His smile. His laugh. His way of looking at her. Had she been too hasty in accepting Noah's proposal? She had made a commitment to him now, and despite the worries in her heart, she still cared for him.

But she was being ridiculous. Her mind couldn't be so easily swayed by Edmund.

Tomorrow would bring the clarity she needed.

Her heart sank when she remembered what her agreement with Mama entailed. She had to spend the day with Edmund. As she stole a glance at his smile, she realized, to her dismay, that she did not dread it.

The group would soon move to the dining room, and Selina suspected the only reason Mama hadn't started already was because of the conversation she wished to prolong between Edmund and Selina. She would likely not be seated near him at dinner, so this might be her only chance to extend the invitation. *It is to appease Mama*, she told herself.

"Because I pity your boredom today," Selina started in a slow voice, "I will grant you the honor of my company tomorrow if you wish to have it. I—I do not have anything else scheduled for the day."

Edmund seemed surprised by her offer, but his eyes piqued with curiosity. "Was it you who just called *me* pompous?"

She glanced up with a smile. "I did not mean to say the honor . . . I meant . . . the *privilege* of my company."

His dimple flickered in and out. "Well, if I should be so fortunate as to receive an invitation from such a prestigious woman, I ought to accept it."

Selina ignored the tug in her stomach, fiddling with her gloves once again. If he knew how much pride she had sacrificed in extending it, he would feel very fortunate indeed. "Very well, Mildred," she whispered. "I will ensure you are not as bored tomorrow as you were today."

Edmund laughed, the sound drowned out by the conversations all around them. "And I will implore you to never call me by that dreadful name again."

"I cannot promise you that." Selina smiled down at her lap, feeling strangely shy. If Mama was right that he was growing attached to her, then it was a cruel thing to encourage him the way her bargain with Mama demanded. He would think his feelings were returned. And he would be wrong.

Wrong.

She told herself as much over and over as they headed to the dining room.

CHAPTER 11

❄

Straightening his cravat, Edmund took one last glance at his reflection to ensure there was nothing amiss before heading down the stairs. He had agreed to meet Selina at noon in the library, but he hadn't the slightest idea of what she had planned for the day. The excitement that barreled through his chest was both thrilling and disconcerting.

Why was he suddenly so eager to spend the day with Selina?

When he had first suggested it, he had done so with the sole intent of keeping her from Skinner, but now his motivations were more selfish. He had found her pretty ever since the first time he had seen her at the Frost Fair—ever since they were children, really, though he never would have admitted that to himself. But now she was far more attractive than she had ever been. Her stubbornness, her laughter, the way she never held her tongue, had all become endearing in the strangest way. She was beautiful and vexing at once, and he had yet to decide if he would rather duel her or kiss her.

He opened the library doors, his gaze falling to where she sat at a table near the window, a nervous smile on her lips. The faint, white light reflecting off the snow illuminated the room just as brightly as the fire burning in the hearth. Selina stood, walking forward to meet him in the middle of the room. She was not nearly as confident approaching him as she had been when they had made the plum pudding. Was it because his efforts were working? He had been so certain before dinner the night before that he was failing, but when she invited him to spend the day with her . . . his confidence was revived. Why else would she wish to spend time with him?

His own heart picked up speed a little as she approached, and he scolded it for doing so. His plan had been to teach *her* what love meant, not to experience anything like it himself. What a mess he was making.

"I didn't know what to plan for today," Selina said in a quiet voice, "so I consulted my mother, who, as you know, is an expert at planning a schedule."

Edmund studied her bashful smile and clear blue eyes, the innocent expression bringing a smile to his own face. "Will we be cooking again?"

"Oh, heavens, no." Selina shook her head fast, her blonde curls swaying. "I would rather run across the frozen river with bare feet."

Edmund tipped his head back, laughing. "Come now, it wasn't so bad. Your cook did all the difficult work." After they had mixed up the ingredients, the cook had insisted that she be responsible for boiling the pudding and hanging it out to dry. "I daresay she didn't trust us at all."

"I do not blame her for that," Selina said, pressing her hand to the side of her face.

"If we aren't cooking, then *are* we running across the river with bare feet? I would pay a great deal of money to see you do that."

Selina laughed. "Then I might finally be able to afford a souvenir."

Edmund watched her cheerful expression and the way the corners of her eyes creased when she wore a genuine smile. If only she knew of her inheritance. If she knew, she would see right through Skinner's schemes. She did have money coming to her. She would soon be able to afford anything she wished for, and she would never be in a position in which she could not afford a cook.

"If you were to purchase this souvenir, which would you choose? The Frost Fair doesn't show any signs of ending soon, you know."

Selina shook her head. "It is silly of me, but I have always had a fascination with tigers, and when I saw a miniature tiger statue at the fair, I confess I did want it. But I would be much smarter to purchase something like it when the fair is over, and the price isn't so high."

"Why tigers?" Edmund meant it as a genuine question, but Selina cast her eyes downward with a smile, as if embarrassed.

"It fascinates me to think that there is an animal like that, much bigger than myself, but much less intelligent, who could destroy me with one swipe of its paw or one movement of its teeth. Something so beautiful roams the earth, yet I will never be able to touch it or be near it without being in danger. They are powerful and fierce and strong, but do they know it? They don't understand exactly what they are, because they lack the intelligence to perceive it."

Edmund listened to the passion behind her description, the excitement in each word. He was reminded of the way his grandmother had often spoken to him of elephants and all the power they held. How Grandmother would have loved to see the elephant that he heard had walked across the River Thames that week. She had always admired that elephants didn't use their strength to harm as predators did. Edmund had never thought so deeply about animals, but after hearing Selina's description, now he would. As he thought about it, he realized Selina was much like the tiger she described, and she, too, did not realize it. Strong and fierce. Beautiful, but too dangerous.

"I think you would have liked to speak with my grandmother," Edmund said. "She was fascinated with all animals. She was partial to elephants. In fact, the statue you mentioned reminds me of a miniature statue of an elephant she has in her home. Rarely did I see her in her chair in the sitting room without picking it up to examine it for dust." A pang of sadness struck his chest as he was reminded that he would never see that sight again, nor would he hear her rasped voice calling a servant and demanding that the elephant's head be dusted for the tenth time.

Selina smiled, tipping her head to one side. "I can imagine myself doing the same when I am advanced in years."

"I too can envision it," Edmund said, chuckling. "With your husband in a nearby chair reading the paper, tired of you pestering the servants, standing to dust the head of your little tiger himself."

He had expected her to smile, but Selina's brow furrowed as

if his words had unsettled her. She likely still assumed that her husband would be Skinner. Did this mean he had succeeded in giving her doubts? Or had something else caused her unease?

"Oh," she said, her expression smoothing over. "I meant to tell you what my mother has planned for us today."

Edmund nodded, hiding his surprise at her abrupt change of subject.

"She thought we might be willing to help her sort the old Christmas decorations she has kept throughout the years. She has far more ribbons than she needs, and tomorrow we will be decorating with greenery as well. We are charged with the task of sorting through and finding the ribbons that are torn or have frayed edges. You will likely be just as bored as you were yesterday." She laughed under her breath.

"Not at all with your conversation to entertain me." He met her gaze. "Although I will need your help. I am not skilled in judging the quality of ribbons."

"It is quite simple." Selina started toward the table, pouring the contents of a nearby box onto the surface. What must have been hundreds of strands of ribbon covered the entire table, piling at least two feet above the surface. Edmund's eyes widened.

"And this is the *second* box," Selina said. "My mother already sorted the first yesterday."

Edmund waited for Selina to sit before taking a seat across from her. He picked up the first ribbon, noting a slight tear on one edge. Selina pointed at the empty box for him to discard it, picking up a ribbon of her own.

"I have always wondered," Selina said, "why you came to visit your grandmother so often if you claimed to hate London."

Edmund moved quickly through the ribbons, examining each briefly. "I never felt like I belonged in London, but I felt like I belonged in my grandmother's house. I felt more loved there than anywhere else. It was a sanctuary of sorts, a place where I felt peace."

Selina watched him, her eyes boring into his with curiosity. "Was your home not the same?"

Edmund shook his head. "It was different. There came to be a competitive spirit between my brother and me. He was the one to inherit everything, and it was his favorite topic of conversation. I was envious, and he knew it, so if we ever argued, he gloated about his privilege. My parents focused their attentions on him, their heir, ensuring he had the very best of everything so he would be suited to manage the estate one day. But here, with my grandmother, I was not pushed aside. I wasn't ignored."

He smiled, his heart stinging once again as he thought of the many months he had spent in London with his grandmother. And now she wanted to give Edmund an inheritance, one Skinner could take away at any moment. How could Selina have been so fooled? As he looked across the table at her now, he realized there was nothing he wouldn't sacrifice to ensure she did not spend her life with such a manipulative man. To ensure she was treasured as she deserved to be. If it came to it, he had to warn her, even if it meant he would lose everything. He wouldn't be able to live with himself otherwise.

Selina gave him a soft smile, one that sent a surge of unfamiliar warmth through his heart. He was not accustomed to being comforted. "Surely you were ignored by *me* many times," she said.

Edmund laughed. She always had seemed aloof toward him, but then, he had been aloof too.

"But I am glad you found such comfort visiting your grandmother," Selina continued. "Have you been reconciled with your brother?"

"Yes." He tossed aside a frayed ribbon. "When I finished school I realized I was happier making a life of my own. Working for it was exactly what I needed. It hadn't ever occurred to me that what I wanted and what I needed could be two separate things. But once I realized it, the two became intertwined. I wanted hard work as much as I needed it."

Selina's brow creased, and she looked down at the table. "In the most favorable situation, that would be the case—what you want and need both aligning."

"I believe that you will come to want anything you truly need." Edmund smiled. "Because you feel the effects of it changing your life for the better, whether you anticipated it or not."

Selina stared at Edmund for a long moment before returning her attention to the ribbons. "When you spoke of your brother and your parents' treatment of you, I found the story quite familiar." She wrapped one end of a ribbon around her finger before unwinding it again. "I have always felt that my mother favored my sister over me. My father died several months before I was born. I once heard my mother say how she prayed for a son who would inherit the house to escape the entailment, and when I was born she was disappointed. I feel as if she . . . blames me for losing the estate. I was never given the privileges Rose was given. Any money spent on lessons were for her. Any new fashions were for her. All praise and love were for her." Selina blinked hard, and

Edmund caught sight of a sheen of tears in her eyes. "It is silly, I know, but it did wear on me to feel like such a disappointment. And now I will disappoint my mother again by my own choice, not something out of my control." She let out a slow breath, as though her confession had removed a visible weight off her shoulders. Her eyes rounded with shock. "Please do not tell anyone I said that. I don't know why I felt the need to tell you at all. I do love my sister, and my mother, so please do not mistake my words."

Edmund shook his head. "Your secrets will always be safe with me, Selina." He paused, choosing his words carefully. "Do you feel that your decision to marry Mr. Skinner has been influenced by that? If your feelings toward your mother were different, would you still be determined to marry him?"

Selina's round eyes stared at him, unblinking, for several seconds before looking away. "Yes, I would still marry him." Her voice was tentative.

There was the thing he had been waiting for. Hesitation.

Snow had begun falling outside the window, and the wind gave a quiet howl as the snowflakes began spiraling wildly, barely visible against the backdrop of the pale grey sky.

"Oh, drat." Selina glanced over her shoulder. "Our afternoon activities also included ice skating. The weather will not allow it now."

"You should consider yourself fortunate. As you know, I am not graceful on ice."

"Nor am I."

Edmund smiled. "All these years, I never would have guessed we were so similar."

Understanding passed between them with a glance before

Selina turned her attention to the window once again. He took the opportunity to study the side of her face. She was obviously troubled. If she had begun to doubt her feelings for Skinner, then he would do all he could to enforce those doubts. There were many reasons he didn't want Selina to marry Skinner, and one that was becoming apparent was that Edmund didn't like the idea of her marrying *anyone*. The thought of any gentleman besides himself making her laugh made his chest tighten with dread . . . and so did the realization that he was well on his way to falling in love with her. *Selina Ellis?* He never would have thought he could grow so fond of her. He had never met another lady like her, and he doubted he ever would.

He bit his lower lip as he considered his next course of action. It wasn't in his nature to give up on something he wanted unless the matter was hopeless. He had never had any hope of inheriting his family's estate, given that he had an elder brother. But he had hope for Selina. She had invited him to spend the day with her; that must have meant something.

What could he do? If his efforts to make her realize that what she felt for Skinner was not love would result in *Edmund* falling in love with her . . . was it worth the cost? His stomach twisted. It was a dangerous game. It seemed Selina was determined not to please her mother.

And nothing would please Mrs. Ellis more than to see her daughter married to Edmund.

His face felt suddenly warm as he sorted through all the strange new emotions in his chest. He was afraid, and that was uncommon for him.

It took him a moment to realize Selina was watching him, her head tipped to one side. "Are you well?"

He nodded, his throat too dry to speak.

"If you don't wish to sort ribbons, you may read a book instead. I'm embarrassed that Mama even gave such a task to a gentleman."

Edmund shook his head before finding his voice. "I actually find it enjoyable." He could be sorting rocks and he would still enjoy sitting across from Selina.

She smiled, resting one elbow on the table as she picked up another ribbon. With Christmas Eve coming the next day, it occurred to him how little time he had. Skinner would be growing impatient by now, especially since Edmund knew of his plan. Selina's trust was delicate, and she was still quite defensive on the subject of her betrothed. Edmund couldn't do anything hasty yet. He had to continue building their friendship and showing her what a true gentleman did when he cared for a lady.

And he did care for her. Far more than he should.

CHAPTER 12

✻

A fresh layer of snow covered the ground on Christmas Eve, still and quiet, contrary to the storm that had caused it to fall the day before. Selina had gotten out of bed early, overwhelmed by thoughts of Edmund and Noah and the choice looming in front of her. Did she have a choice? She had committed to marry Noah, and she was certain that if she had as much time to spend with him as she did with Edmund that she would remember her feelings for him. But at the moment, thoughts of Noah were far less enjoyable to dwell on than thoughts of Edmund. It troubled her enough to keep her from getting any sleep the night before.

Every Christmas Eve, Mama enlisted all the help she could find to decorate the house with greenery and ribbons. This year was no different. Once Selina and Edmund had finished sorting through the ribbons the day before, they had spent most of the afternoon in the library, talking and laughing about insignificant things that somehow felt significant. Selina hadn't wanted to leave the drawing room after dinner because it meant their conversation would have to end. She never would have assumed they could be anything resembling friends, but that's what he was to her now. A friend.

Only a friend.

Instilling that thought in her mind had been her mission all night, and that was why she hadn't slept.

The thought simply did not want to stick.

Today, Mama had invited the Perrys to assist in the decorating, as she and Mrs. Perry had been planning their decorations together. Mama had likely gone to a great deal of work to ensure their house would be more thoroughly decorated, and she didn't want Mrs. Perry to miss that fact. Mama refused to give the task to any servants, claiming that it was her favorite tradition of all.

A surge of excitement entered Selina's stomach as she thought of the day ahead. Perhaps Edmund would look at her first when he walked into the drawing room again. If he did, then she might finally have to believe her mother about his attachment.

She scolded herself as she walked down the stairs, straightening the pendant at her neck. Why should she hope for such a thing? It was cruel of her. She would have to reject him if he carried on like that.

A smile tugged on her lips as she walked toward the drawing room. She paused outside the door, brow creasing. A deep voice was speaking from inside, muffled slightly by the door. After a few seconds, she recognized it as Edmund's. Smoothing back her curls, she walked through the doorway. She took one step, making sure to glance first at Mama so she wouldn't assume Selina was developing an attachment to Edmund because she *was not*. She drove the thought deeper into her mind as she allowed herself one glance in his direction.

He was sitting on his usual spot on the sofa, looking to Miss Perry with a smile, who was seated beside him. Her voice was too quiet for Selina to decipher her words. Edmund nodded as she spoke, completely distracted by whatever it was that she was saying. He didn't even glance up as Selina walked into the room, or as she took a seat beside her mother. Selina swallowed her disappointment, putting on a nonchalant smile as Mrs. Perry cast a smug one her way. Did she think Selina was vying for Edmund's attention? Preposterous.

Selina watched Miss Perry as she covered her lips with a giggle. What had Edmund said to make her laugh? Did he find her conversation amusing as well? Slowly, the smile began to melt off of Selina's face like a snowflake after landing on warm skin. Perhaps Edmund would develop an attachment to Miss Perry. Selina had even once wanted that to happen—she had been prepared to trap him in an engagement with Miss Perry if it meant he would leave Selina alone.

They were sitting far too close to one another. Miss Perry had an entire three inches between herself and the side of the sofa. She could have easily filled it, but her leg was nearly touching Edmund's instead.

"I do not like it either," Mama whispered in Selina's ear.

She jumped, whirling to face Mama. "What do you mean?"

"You know precisely what I mean." Mama's eye twitched in Edmund and Miss Perry's direction. She gave a fake laugh to disguise the subject of their conversation. "Not to worry. She came to sit by him first. I suspect he was hoping you would take the seat beside him."

Relief flooded Selina's chest, but she ignored it. Why did she care so much? She put on an indifferent expression. "Oh, Mama, do you still believe I care about such things? Miss Perry can have him, and I will not care one bit."

Mama glowered. "Please do not speak such nonsense. I can see by the way you have been watching them with the eyes of an abandoned hound that you will care a great deal more than *one bit*."

A flush of heat came to Selina's cheeks before she gained control of her embarrassment. Is that what this was? Had she truly begun to care for Edmund more than what was appropriate given her . . . engagement to Noah? How could she care for two men at once? That did not seem proper in the slightest.

"I am not looking at them like an *abandoned hound*," Selina whispered through her teeth. She raised her voice just enough so Mrs. Perry would overhear. "I was simply admiring Miss Perry's dress. The green does much for her complexion."

Mrs. Perry cast a satisfied smile in her daughter's direction. "Yes, I have always told her to wear green more often. And think of all the greenery that will surround her as we decorate today! She will be positively radiant."

"Indeed." Selina examined Miss Perry. She was quite pretty, and she was taller than Selina. Did Edmund find tall women more attractive than short women? Selina was somewhere between tall and short, but Miss Perry was decidedly tall. And she had auburn hair, which was lovely for how uncommon it was. As she weighed Miss Perry's strengths and weaknesses in her mind, she made sure not to stare at her for too long. She could not have Mama or Mrs. Perry thinking anything ridiculous.

"Well, I think it is time to begin," Mama said. "Shall we start with this room? I have been most excited to adorn the mantel."

Mama's voice finally broke Miss Perry's gaze and pulled it away from Edmund's face. They both turned to face her, and Edmund's eyes found Selina's. By the way he greeted her with a small smile, it seemed he truly hadn't noticed her entrance at all.

The group stood, and Mrs. Perry tapped her chin. "There are several rooms in need of decorating. Perhaps we could divide our group and achieve more in a shorter time."

"That is a very good idea, Mama," Miss Perry said. Selina might have been imagining it, but Miss Perry seemed to move closer to Edmund.

"How shall we divide?" Mrs. Perry continued before receiving Mama's approval. "Perhaps Mrs. Ellis and I will decorate this room . . . " She glanced at Selina in a way that told Selina her presence there was a severe inconvenience. "And the other three, I suppose, may begin in the entry."

Selina met Edmund's gaze quickly before tearing it away.

"That will be a perfect arrangement," Miss Perry agreed. "Mrs. Ellis and Miss Ellis know the house best, so they ought not to be grouped together."

"Sir Edmund knows the house quite well also, as he has been our guest for several days." Mama's voice was pointed to remind Miss Perry of Selina's advantage. Why Mama continued inviting the Perrys was a mystery. She seemed to revel in the rivalry, but only when she felt certain of her own victory.

Selina found it all very tiresome.

Miss Perry watched Selina carefully as she approached Edmund. "Let us hope the ribbons we sorted are to my mother's satisfaction today," Selina said.

Edmund's dark curls fell over his forehead, a smile hovering at the edges of his eyes. "If they are not, I dare not imagine the consequences."

Selina gave a quiet laugh, which was quickly stamped out by Miss Perry's sharp gaze. "Shall we be going to the entry hall?"

Selina nodded, casting one more glance at Edmund before leading the way out the door.

❄

"How fortunate we are to have Sir Edmund in our group," Miss Perry said as she walked at Edmund's side. She stared up at him, just as she had been since arriving in the drawing room. Edmund shifted uncomfortably.

"I daresay he is tall enough to reach all the places we will wish to decorate," Miss Perry continued with a laugh.

Selina cast a critical gaze over her shoulder at him as they passed through the short hallway that led to the entry hall. "He is not nearly tall enough if I wished to decorate the ceiling," she said in an offhand voice.

Edmund watched with a smile as she walked with quick steps into the entry hall, only sparing him the one glance. She always did try to keep him humble.

"I've never met a man tall enough for that," Selina said. "Have you, Miss Perry?"

Miss Perry turned to Edmund with a shrill laugh. "Most certainly not!"

He took a slight step to the side to put more distance between her laughter and his ear. Her demeanor had changed drastically since the last time he had seen her at the Frost Fair, and he believed Mrs. Perry was to blame for that. The competitive nature between Mrs. Ellis and Mrs. Perry was obvious, and it was no surprise Mrs. Perry had sent her daughter to pursue him that day. The moment they entered the room she had claimed the seat beside him, speaking constantly about everything from the color of her new pelisse to the things she had witnessed at the fair.

"I am certain Sir Edmund could find a way to hang the ribbons as high as the ceiling." Miss Perry smiled up at him. "He is quite strong, you know."

Selina's shoulders seemed to stiffen as she turned toward them, her eyes darting between Edmund and Miss Perry. She took a long glance at Edmund's arms. "Actually, I did not know that, but I thank you for enlightening me." Selina met Edmund's gaze with a smirk before turning her attention to the box of ribbons and the side table that had been set with the greenery and twine needed to decorate the banister. Was Selina teasing him now?

"Well—" Miss Perry stuttered. "I suppose I do not *know* that he is strong, but he has the appearance of someone quite strong."

"What has given you that indication?" Selina's eyes were round with innocence, but Edmund detected the motive behind her question. She wished to make Edmund uncomfortable.

Miss Perry turned toward him, her thoughtful expression drawing her brows together. "Well, his arms are quite large, but when he escorted me I noted that they are not soft like a loaf of bread. The feeling of his arm was more akin to a roast beast, indicating muscle tissue, which aids in physical strength."

Selina's gaze darted to Edmund's, her lips pressing together in a manner that he had come to recognize meant she was holding back laughter. She had succeeded in her aim.

He was certainly uncomfortable.

"Are you quite certain, Miss Perry?" Selina asked. "I thought the opposite. Even now, looking at his arms, I am reminded of two loaves of bread I saw in the kitchen this morning. Personally, I prefer men to have arms like that. There is little else I like more than freshly baked bread."

Edmund scoffed in disbelief. *Bread?* That was not what a man wanted to hear. "I have never given such thought to my arms, so I thank you both for your assessments." He smiled first at Miss Perry, then at Selina, who was taking far too much pleasure in his discomfort.

After nearly an hour of hanging the holly and evergreen boughs and arranging them with red and gold ribbons on the banister, they started back to the drawing room where Mrs. Ellis and Mrs. Perry were awaiting them. Edmund had hardly had any chance to speak with Selina with Miss Perry's constant prattle, and Selina hadn't seemed inclined to speak over her. Edmund had been as polite as he could, listening to the many things Miss Perry had to say with smiles and nods. Now that they were walking back to the drawing room, she looped her hand through his arm, holding it with a grip so tight, a loaf of bread would have flattened. Selina trailed behind, her feet clicking softly on the marble floor.

A few paces beyond the open doorway, Mrs. Ellis and Mrs. Perry stood, observing their approach with wide eyes. Mrs. Ellis's gaze flickered upward before settling on Edmund again, a crease on her brow.

What was the matter? Had she seen the pained expression he wore at having his arm flattened?

As they walked closer to the room, he caught sight of the source of Mrs. Ellis's dismay and Mrs. Perry's apparent delight, hanging just inside the doorway.

A kissing bough.

CHAPTER 13

How many times would she giggle like that? Selina trailed behind Miss Perry and Edmund as they headed back to the drawing room, still carrying the shears she had used to cut the greenery. She had always been taught to keep her laughter to an appropriate volume, a lesson Miss Perry had obviously never received. And why on earth was Miss Perry holding Edmund's arm so tightly? Was she admiring its roasted meat texture? Edmund hadn't seemed to mind her company, though, always listening and smiling at her constant prattle.

As they approached the doorway, Selina caught sight of Mama, who was scowling as Edmund and Miss Perry approached, her eyes flickering up to the ceiling as if a spider or some other unsightly creature was hovering there.

It took Selina only a short moment to see the disagreeable thing that was hanging just above where Edmund and Miss Perry now stood. Selina's chest tightened as she watched the look of delight on Mrs. Perry's face. Had she placed the kissing bough there, knowing her daughter would be caught under it with Edmund? If so, that must have been the source of the rage building in Mama's features.

Selina stopped several paces back, her heart thudding.

"You two are beneath the kissing bough!" Mrs. Perry exclaimed. "I need not explain what tradition demands."

Miss Perry gave another of her giggles, turning to face Edmund. "Oh, dear, how embarrassing to share a kiss with such an audience."

Edmund stood with an unreadable expression, glancing at Selina. When he turned his attention back to Miss Perry, she rose on her toes in one quick motion. Being as tall as she was, it was no difficulty for her to reach him as she pressed her lips to his.

Mrs. Perry cheered, clapping her hands and laughing. Selina tore her gaze away, turning on her heel, her feet carrying her with long strides back to the entry hall. Her heart pounded as she turned toward the staircase, bounding up two stairs at a time. When she was safely behind the door of her bedchamber, she paused to take a breath.

Her lungs felt heavy, and so did the stone that had settled in her stomach.

She jumped when a knock sounded on her door. Had Mama come up to see if she was unwell? She couldn't let her know how that kiss had affected her. Why *had it* affected her? Edmund could kiss whomever he pleased, whenever and wherever he pleased. It meant nothing to Selina. *Be calm. Be indifferent.* She set down the shears and searched for something else she could hold so it would appear she had come upstairs for a purpose. After a short search, she found a pair of gloves and nonchalantly began slipping them on as she opened the door.

Her heart leaped as she glanced up. It wasn't Mama. "Edmund?"

He appeared to be slightly out of breath, as though he had run up the stairs as quickly as she had. His dark curls were slightly mussed. Had that been Miss Perry's doing? Selina blocked the thought from her mind.

"What are you doing up here?" Selina asked in a nonchalant voice. She swallowed hard, looking at anything but his face.

"I wondered why you ran away." Edmund's chest rose and fell quickly. "The kissing bough—"

Selina scoffed, stopping him. "I didn't run. I hurried away, yes, but that was because . . . my hands were quite cold." She nodded toward the gloves she held.

Edmund took a step closer. "I did not know the kissing bough was there until it was too late, and I certainly didn't know Miss Perry would kiss me."

"Do you think me distressed over it?" Selina laughed, tucking away the emotions she had been feeling as she hurried up the stairs. You may kiss whomever you wish. I was merely . . . surprised. I thought you did not wish to be ensnared into marrying her."

"I did not wish to kiss Miss Perry." He shook his head, his eyes wide. "And I have no wish to further our acquaintance."

A small spark of hope entered Selina's chest, but she extinguished it. Pain and inexplicable feelings still festered too close to her heart. "Well, was it enjoyable?" She avoided his gaze.

Edmund scoffed with disbelief. "She forced it upon me. I turned away quickly and worried about where you had gone. I worried if you were upset by the—the ordeal."

He hadn't seemed opposed to Miss Perry's company all day.

And she was obviously pretty. What man would object so heartily to a kiss from any woman even half so pretty? Selina's heart pounded, spreading an ache through her entire body. Her defenses continued to rise. The only way to manage such feelings was to act indifferent. "You forget that I am engaged to Mr. Skinner. Why should I be upset?" It was true. She felt disloyal to Noah for feeling so envious of Miss Perry. Perhaps the only reason for her envy was because she wished Noah would kiss her. Yes, that must have been it. She gathered her confidence and met Edmund's gaze, holding her chin high.

Edmund did not seem convinced by her act. He took another step closer, one that caused her heart to flip and her feet to stumble backward. His blue eyes bore into hers. "Whether you are upset or not, I wanted to come up here to see if you were well."

Selina caught her breath, nodding fast. "I am well. I have never been more well, in fact." She clamped her mouth shut before she could say anything else strange. "And now that I have my gloves, I can come back downstairs." She made to walk forward, but Edmund didn't move.

She slowly raised her gaze to his, her heart thudding like a wild bird against her ribs.

"Are you certain it didn't upset you?" His voice was tentative, but his gaze was more direct than she had ever seen it.

Selina took a deep breath, doing all she could to ignore the way his eyes lowered briefly to her lips. How could she admit that seeing him with Miss Perry that day had bothered her so greatly? How could she admit that seeing them kiss had made her feel ill, even if it had only occurred because of a silly tradition and Mrs. Perry's scheming? She couldn't tell him.

"Yes." She met his gaze with great effort before focusing on the buttons of his jacket instead. Talking to a row of buttons was much easier. "I am certain." When she gathered the courage to look up at him again, she was surprised by his expression. He looked . . . disappointed.

"Well, I am glad you are well," he said. "I would never wish to upset you."

Selina searched his face, the intensity of his gaze trapping her. She couldn't look away. An invisible force drew her to him, and she realized there was little she wouldn't do or say to erase the dejection from his gaze. She would even kiss him herself.

She banished the idea from her mind instantly, guilt driving deep into her chest. How could she have such a thought when she was engaged to someone else? In *love* with someone else? But that word, *love,* clattered through her mind like it didn't belong, resulting in an echo of uncertainty.

Before she could question what it meant, Edmund took her hand in his, the one she had yet to cover with a glove. Her breath caught in her throat as he glanced down at it, his dark lashes hiding his eyes from her view. "How interesting," he said in a quiet voice, his thumb tracing over the top of her hand. His eyes met hers. "Your hands are not cold at all." He released her fingers before taking a step back.

She swallowed, her throat too dry to speak.

He did not believe her.

He could easily see that she had not run up the stairs to fetch her gloves. She ran up the stairs because she was afraid— very afraid—that Edmund would fall in love with someone else. She ran up the stairs because she couldn't bear to see him kiss Miss Perry. And she ran up the stairs because she recognized a flame within her chest, a spark that had grown throughout the time she had spent with Edmund, burning brighter with each passing moment. It was easy to extinguish a flame burning on the end of a wick, but the candle had capsized, catching and spreading until it had become something she couldn't control. Her feelings were not submissive, no matter how much she tried to tame them.

Edmund had become dear to her. That was all she knew. And she didn't want to lose him—especially not to Miss Perry.

Before Selina could concoct a story to explain the warmth of her hands, Edmund gave her a gentle smile, one that set her racing thoughts at ease, if only for a moment. "We should go back to the drawing room. Your mother was worried about your absence."

Selina closed her bedchamber door, following Edmund toward the stairs. Edmund turned toward her with a reassuring smile. "You may walk in ahead of me if you wish. I would not expect you to hope to be caught under the kissing bough with me."

Selina's cheeks grew warm. All this talk of kissing was beginning to make her vastly uncomfortable. Who had invented such a tradition? It was improper and until today, Mama had never decorated with kissing boughs. The servants had been known to hang them in their own quarters, but never in the public areas of the house where unsuspecting guests might be caught beneath them. "That is very considerate of you. I wonder where such manners were when Miss Perry was on your arm." Selina stopped herself, her eyes widening. What was wrong with her?

One corner of Edmund's mouth lifted in a smile as they reached the bottom of the stairs. "It seems the rivalry between your mother and Mrs. Perry extends to their children." He gave her a pointed look, a teasing glint in his eyes.

Selina's face heated again, and she shook her head, laughing as if she actually found his words humorous. "Miss Perry is not my rival. I was only concerned for her heart. She may very well be falling in love with you and I do not know where your feelings for her stand."

The drawing room was at the end of the short hallway, so Selina walked a few paces ahead to avoid being caught in the doorway with him.

"My feelings?" Edmund met her gaze as she glanced over her shoulder. "My feelings are otherwise engaged." His jaw tightened as he turned his attention to the floor.

Selina's gaze lingered on him as she walked, and she nearly crashed into Mama as she met her in the doorway, pulling her hastily inside. "You will not believe what I have done." Mama's voice was a harsh whisper. Mrs. Perry and her daughter sat on the other side of the room, watching eagerly as Edmund stepped through the door. Rather than take the open seat beside Miss Perry, Edmund chose the chair by the fire.

"What is it?" Selina whispered, her brow furrowing at Mama's concerned expression.

With a sigh, Mama turned her back to the other guests for long enough to whisper without being seen or heard. "I hung the kissing bough in the hopes of catching you and Sir Edmund beneath it. When Mrs. Perry discovered my plan, she made the assumption that her daughter would be the one walking through at his side."

Selina crossed her arms. "And she was right."

Mama pressed a hand to her chest. "*Indeed.*" Her eyes

narrowed. "I am just as distressed over it as you are. I was certain it would be you and Edmund walking through the doorway together, and now that he has kissed Miss Perry, he will likely fall in love with her and I shall never have him as my son-in-law."

"Mama!" Selina scolded in a whisper, glancing behind her to ensure Edmund hadn't overheard. "Please do not say such things aloud." She paused. "And I am not distressed."

Mama sighed. "However . . . I did find it quite gallant how he ran off after you like that. The moment Miss Perry released him from her insufferable grip he started in your direction."

Selina followed Mama's gaze to Edmund, careful to not be caught staring. He was turned away from her, watching the flames flickering in the hearth.

"No matter what Mrs. Perry wishes to believe . . . " Mama said. "I daresay he wished it had been you with him under the kissing bough."

Selina shook her head, unwilling to believe such a thing, despite all the signs that told her it might have been true. "Even if he wished for it, I would not have kissed him. I am not nearly as improper as Miss Perry."

Mama clicked her tongue quietly. "I would not be so certain. There is no better time than Christmastide for wishes to be granted."

"Mama!"

Without listening, Mama turned away, returning to her guests. Selina stayed by her mother's side, too vexed by the Perrys and too conflicted toward Edmund to choose any of them as companions. The decorating was almost finished, so it wouldn't be long before Selina could return to her room for a time. Thankfully, the Perrys would not be joining them for Christmas

Eve dinner, but that also meant it would just be Mama, Selina, and Edmund sitting around the table.

Selina comforted herself with the fact that tomorrow was Christmas Day. She would see Noah in the churchyard and perhaps find the answers her heart sought.

CHAPTER 14

❄

"Mr. Skinner will be awaiting me outside," Selina said as she walked out of the church at Edmund's side. Wrapped up in all her warm layers, she looked unfairly endearing, her smooth cheeks flushed from the cold. She had hardly spoken to him since the day before, avoiding his gaze and retreating back to the way she had been before they had established any sort of friendship between them. Even if she was relaying such terrible news, he was simply glad she was speaking to him.

Edmund's gaze darted around the churchyard, and he fell back a pace. "Skinner is here?"

"Do not let my mother overhear," Selina whispered. "I imagine she will remain distracted by all the people here, but if she looks for me, will you distract her?" Her clear eyes stared up at him, the color even more striking against the white snow all around them. "I—I need to speak to him." She wrung her fingers together.

Edmund watched the signs of nervousness in her, hope rising in his chest. Had she finally seen sense? Would she tell him she no longer wished to marry him? As pleased as he was with that idea, a pang of worry struck him. Would Skinner find a way to blame Edmund and burn the will? He had to hide before he was seen with Selina.

"What is the matter?" Selina asked, likely noting the way Edmund's brow had creased with worry.

"Nothing at all." He glanced around again before nodding. "And yes, I will keep your mother from finding you." He had been doing all he could to gain Selina's trust, but the day before, though he hadn't intended to, he seemed to have lost a bit of it. Miss Perry's kiss had meant nothing to him, and he had done nothing to encourage it, yet Selina had obviously been hurt by it. That alone was encouraging, but he also hated to see her upset. "I will wait back here," he said. "I believe your mother is still inside." Edmund paused. "Where are you meeting him?"

Selina pointed discreetly behind the church where few people ever ventured. "It will have to be brief. He is likely already there awaiting me."

Edmund stiffened, taking several paces back. "You ought to be going, then."

Selina seemed reluctant to move, a line between her eyebrows. It was as if she missed the time when Edmund had done all in his power to keep her from Skinner. It was almost as if she wished he would. "Very well," she said in a soft voice. "I will return shortly."

Edmund watched as she started in the direction she had pointed. He waited until she was almost out of view before turning on his heel. With long strides, he walked around the opposite side of the church, stopping once he reached the outer left wall. He pressed his shoulder against it, peering around the corner of the church just enough so he could see the yard beyond it.

Selina stood with her arms crossed as Mr. Skinner approached her, removing his hat. Edmund listened closely, but he was unable to catch their conversation from where he stood, and to move closer he would risk being seen. He kept his eyes fixed on Selina and the way she held her arms wrapped around herself rather than Skinner as she had when he had first witnessed them together.

Edmund crossed his own arms, a deep chill running over his skin as snow began falling. As he observed the conversation, Selina seemed to relax her posture, even smiling up at Skinner once or twice. A pang of jealousy drove its way into Edmund's heart, and his hope began to diminish. Was he a fool to think he could change her mind? Did she really care deeply enough for Skinner to follow through with the marriage, even at the expense of her station and her mother's respect? As Edmund considered his own feelings for Selina, he realized he would be willing to give up such things if it meant he could spend each day with her. If her feelings for Skinner extended so far, then she no longer seemed like such a fool.

She had been *fooled*, but that did not make her a fool. Edmund had been fooled too. He had allowed himself to believe that Selina cared for him as more than a friend, a face from the past, or a guest at her mother's house.

When Selina stepped away from Skinner, Edmund watched them part ways. Distracted as he was by Selina, he didn't realize Skinner was walking directly toward him.

He scrambled away from the side of the church, straightening his hat and walking in the opposite direction. He had almost made it to the front of the church before he risked a careful glance behind him from beneath the brim of his hat. Standing near the place Edmund had just been, was Skinner, his gaze pointed in Edmund's direction. The distance between them and the falling snow might have been enough to make Edmund unrecognizable, but his stomach twisted with dread as he realized he was standing in fresh snow. Skinner would see his footprints and know how close he had just been. He would know Edmund had been watching them.

Edmund walked casually toward the front of the church, finding Mrs. Ellis and Selina reunited on the front steps. He held his breath, afraid to glance back and find Skinner following him.

"Where have you been, Sir Edmund?" Mrs. Ellis cast him a bright smile. "I simply cannot allow you to leave our sides on such a happy day as this." She cast her gaze up at the sky. "If only the weather had allowed Rose to travel into London today. How much happier still the day could be. I am never so happy as when Rose comes to visit."

Edmund never thought he would be glad that the weather had remained so treacherous for travel. His work in London wasn't through yet, and if the snow melted, he would lose his excuse to stay.

Edmund met Selina's gaze, holding it for several seconds. There was something different in her eyes, and he spent the walk home trying to decipher what it was. It wasn't until he walked through the front doors of the house that he recognized it.

Regret.

It hadn't been there before she spoke with Skinner, so he could be the only one to blame for the regret in her eyes. The moment they walked through the doors, Selina took off her hat, pelisse, and gloves, and started up the stairs, moving almost as quickly as she had the day before when Miss Perry had kissed Edmund.

Edmund waited at the base of the stairs as Mrs. Ellis removed to the kitchen to check on the Christmas feast preparations, debating over whether or not Selina wanted to be followed.

❄

Why hadn't she said it? Selina sat on the edge of her bed, rubbing her forehead with two fingers. Noah had relayed his plans to her regarding their elopement, and all she had been able to think of was Edmund. Her heart stung as regret threatened to consume her. Why was it so difficult to let go of Noah? She had been dreaming of him for so many months, mistaking the feelings in her heart for love. But now it was clear that all she had ever felt for him was fascination. Attraction. And a bit of fixation. She had meant to tell him that day that she no longer wished to marry him, at least not yet.

Her heart pounded fast. If she really loved Noah, the opportunity to spend her life with him would have been worth any cost. She would be feeling eager and excited and overjoyed to hear that there was a plan in place to make that possible. But all she felt was empty and afraid. The emptiness she now felt left room for the things Edmund had been telling her about Skinner all along. What if he was not to be trusted? But what reason could he have for marrying her if he did not truly care for her?

He had told her he did many times, and she had nothing to offer besides her own heart. So what else could it be?

She laid back with a groan, throwing her arms above her. Why must her heart be so difficult to understand?

A knock sounded on her door again, making her heart leap. As she rose to answer it, she prepared herself for the possibility that it could be Edmund standing there again. Taking a deep breath, she pulled it open. Despite her preparations, she was still surprised to see his face.

"I am sorry to disturb you," he said, glancing down either side of the hall as if worried over being seen outside her room. "But I wanted to inquire about your conversation with Mr. Skinner. You seemed . . . somewhat troubled. What did he say to you?"

Selina steadied herself with a breath. She had already lied to him yesterday, and he had seen straight through it. How could she lie to him again? He could read her emotions as if they were written out on her face, and perhaps they were. "I don't wish to speak of Mr. Skinner," Selina said, pushing aside her worry. She didn't want Edmund to be concerned for her. This was her life and her emotions to sort through. He had burdened himself with her affairs too much already, and there was no place for such heavy things on Christmas. "My mother will be quite busy preparing to receive her guests tonight," Selina continued. She planned her words carefully. "Would you join me in the library for a game of chess? It seems just the sort of activity for a day like today."

A slight smile curved his lips, his eyes soft. "I hope you are prepared to lose."

"I have never lost."

Edmund chuckled, following her to the library. The heaviness in Selina's chest faded as she played chess with Edmund, and she was not even upset when he managed to win the game. The quiet warmth of the library and Edmund's company eased the ache in her chest, leaving room for laughter and joy and the sorts of things one was meant to feel on Christmas.

"You must have cheated to have won so easily," Selina said in an offhand voice, picking up a pawn and turning it over in her hand.

Edmund exhaled sharply in disbelief before a smile claimed his expression. "You simply underestimated my skill."

She leaned one elbow on the table. "Or perhaps I did not play my best."

His eyes flew up to hers. "If that is the case then I demand another match."

In truth, she had played to win, but Edmund did not need to know that he was really as skilled as he was. He was pompous enough already. Selina smiled as she gathered up her pieces.

They spoke less during their second match, too focused to communicate in anything but glances. Perhaps it was Edmund's ability to read her that made his second victory so effortless, or perhaps it was that she wasn't as skilled at chess as she had thought. If he was worse at keeping his features neutral and unreadable, then she might have been able to guess his next move.

Selina sat back with a sigh, narrowing her eyes at him. "You are cruel to watch me lose twice on Christmas Day." She rubbed her arms, a sudden chill seeping through her skin.

Edmund must have noticed, for he stood, gesturing to the nearby fire. She followed him to the chairs in front of it, half-hoping he would move them farther apart before sitting down.

He didn't.

Once she had settled into her chair, Edmund turned slightly toward her. His smile had faded into a look of curiosity. The fire crackled, warming her toes. She hadn't realized how cold they had been.

"May I ask you a question?" Edmund said. "I do not require an answer, but you would appease my curiosity greatly if you gave one."

Selina nodded, her throat suddenly parched.

"Has Mr. Skinner ever told you why he chose to marry you?"

His words fell hollow on her ears, and she searched for any instance that would match what he described. "Not outrightly, I suppose." Selina extended her hands closer to the fire, watching as the sparks diminished under the wood.

"Have you given much thought to that question before now?" Edmund met her gaze.

Selina felt suddenly self-conscious. Why was he asking? Did he believe it so unlikely that a man would admire her enough to propose? "I have not," Selina said.

Edmund leaned forward in his chair, drawing her gaze back to him. "Don't you find it curious that he would ask you to marry him at all?"

Selina turned to face him. "It offends me that you are so *baffled*."

Edmund frowned. "Baffled?"

"You are baffled that any man would admire me enough to

marry me, even a man beneath my station. I do not need to know *why* he would wish to marry me, only that he does."

Edmund shook his head at the ground, and a muscle jumped in his clenched jaw. "I am far from baffled over why any man would wish to marry you." His eyes found hers, shadowed by the curls on his forehead and the harsh light from the fire. Her heart pounded as he leaned his arm not on his own chair, but on hers. "But I am baffled that your own betrothed has not told you himself. Could he not take a moment to explain how you reign his thoughts? How he wishes to be near you always, and never be parted from you?"

Edmund cast his gaze downward briefly, his frustration seeming to rise as he spoke. "If he were to do it right, he would tell you how your laugh enchants him, how your eyes hold him captive, and of the many moments he has spent hoping you would one day be his. He might even tell you that there is no clear explanation for why he loves you, but simply that he does—that his love is built from every part of you, good and bad, every moment, and every word. If he were to make a list of the reasons, it would be too extensive, and it wouldn't properly encompass the complexity of what he feels." Edmund's words stopped abruptly. His eyes searched her face. He seemed to be looking for something important. He was so close, leaning on the arm of her chair as he was. Selina could hardly breathe.

The feelings pulsing through her chest were unfamiliar, and she knew without a doubt that if those words had come from Noah she would not have felt like *this*. She was on a cliff, torn between staying and falling.

And it was Edmund, not Mr. Skinner waiting to catch her if she fell.

Her gaze lowered from Edmund's eyes to his lips, fighting the longing to take his face between her hands and kiss him just as Miss Perry had . . . perhaps for a little longer.

Had he leaned closer? Selina drew a breath, her heart leaping as she caught the way his own gaze traced across her face and settled on her mouth. His brows drew together, a sign that he was fighting the same odd desire she felt. A kissing bough would have made it more proper, but there were none to be found.

Before she could be as bold as Miss Perry, Edmund tore his gaze away, and, in one swift motion, stood and turned toward the door before facing her again. "I invite you to ask him," Edmund said.

Selina found her voice, her pulse still thrumming in her ears. "Who?"

"Ask Skinner why he wishes to marry you."

She nodded, her voice evading her, which seemed to give Edmund leave to exit the room. She would have asked Edmund why he was so troubled, just as he had asked her that day, but the answer was obvious. If he felt the same things she did . . . then he would be troubled knowing she was still engaged to another.

As she stared into the fireplace, she vowed that the next time she saw Mr. Skinner she would tell him she no longer wished to marry him. And after that, she would do something even more difficult.

She would admit to Edmund that she was wrong.

❄

Selina made her way to the drawing room early that night. She had taken great care to look elegant, even asking her maid for a hair arrangement she hadn't yet attempted. Selina had been pleased with the result, though it did nothing to ease the worry inside her. She sat alone, listening to the ticking of the clock as she adjusted the skirts of her ivory evening gown.

The sun had already gone down and the candles in the drawing room had been lit, filling the space with a warmth that belied the coldness in her chest. The door opened abruptly, and she stiffened, expecting it to be Edmund entering. Instead, it was Mama, a hand pressed to her chest and tears glistening in her eyes.

"What is wrong?" Selina's heart pounded with dread until a smile broke over Mama's cheeks.

"Rose! She is here!"

Selina stood, surprised by the surge of joy that struck her. "In London? How?"

Mama rushed to the drawing room window, picking up a candle on her way. Her blue taffeta sleeves rustled loudly as she pulled back the drapes. "The footmen are bringing their trunks in now." Mama squealed with delight. "How dare she surprise us like this? Will I have enough food?"

Mama had always overestimated the food to have prepared for the Christmas Day Feast, so Selina had no doubt that both Rose and her husband would be well fed. Mama had also invited her distant cousins and their families, the Godwins and Setons, to join them, as many families neglected to even celebrate Christmastide in London—at least not with as much care as Mama did.

"Are you certain it is her?" Selina asked. It could have been any of the other guests.

"I would recognize my own daughter." Mama scowled before

rustling her way out the door again. "Make haste!" she said. "Come greet your sister."

Selina followed, happy for a distraction from her present concerns. And she did miss Rose, despite everything.

She stepped into the entry hall at the same moment Rose stepped through the front doors. Even the arduous travels had done nothing to diminish her beauty. She cast Selina a wide smile, her blue eyes sparkling as she clasped her hands. "Selina, how long it has been."

Rose's husband, Mr. Vaughan, walked through behind her, a cold breeze following him. He was of average height and build, and not nearly as handsome as his wife. Rose had married him for his wealth above any other attractions. Thankfully he was an amiable man and treated Rose with respect and generosity, which was all she had ever aspired to. Selina shivered as the cold air seeped through her arms, wishing she had long sleeves like Rose's to block out the cold.

"What made you come here with such dangerous weather?" Selina asked. "When did you decide to make the journey?"

Rose glanced at her husband with an expression that could only be described as a half-smile, half-grimace. "My husband's family is dreadfully boring during Christmastide. I begged him to bring me here and he finally obliged. We would have arrived several days ago if the roads had not been so treacherous."

Selina gaped at her. "Well, I am glad you've arrived safely."

"As am I." Rose cast her gaze about the entry hall with a sigh. "What an interesting way to have decorated this year. I wish I had been here to help. The evergreen boughs are far too frequently placed. I would have used them sparingly to allow more space for ribbons."

Selina did not look fondly on the memories of decorating the day before, so she did not mind Rose's criticism. The abundance of evergreen boughs had all been Miss Perry's idea. If it had been she and Edmund decorating, perhaps the task would have been completed to Rose's satisfaction.

As if materialized by her thoughts of him, Edmund stepped out from the bottom of the staircase. He was dressed in his formal black jacket and pure white cravat, his hair combed neatly and his eyes striking, even from a distance. His gaze took her in first, and she didn't have the strength or desire to look away. It was Christmas Day. She could do as she wished.

He turned his attention to Rose and her husband next, a smile of recognition pulling on his lips.

"Mr. Sharp?" Rose said in a tone of surprise. "Have my eyes deceived me, or is that truly you?"

"It is Sir Edmund now," Mama corrected, her voice dripping with pride as if she had some claim on the honor of his knighthood. "He is our guest until the roads become safer to travel, though I would not object to him staying even longer than that." Mama grinned.

Rose cast a glance in Selina's direction, a sly smile on her lips. "I see. Well, I recall Edmund has always been a very amiable man."

Selina looked at the floor, embarrassed by the sly smiles passing between Mama and Rose.

"I would not trespass on your hospitality longer than necessary, Mrs. Ellis." Edmund smiled, catching Selina's gaze. "My visit was unexpected enough already."

"Nonsense! You could not trespass even if you stayed for the rest of your life." Mama laughed, casting one of her sly smiles at Selina.

"When are the other guests expected to arrive?" Selina blurted, her face growing hot.

Mama rambled on about their arrival, but Selina hardly heard her. She could feel Edmund's gaze on the side of her face, and she could focus on little else.

After sitting in the drawing room for several minutes while Rose and Mr. Vaughan changed for dinner, it was time to move to the dining room. According to the rankings of the guests, Edmund was expected to escort Miss Godwin, who was a distant cousin of Selina's.

Near the end of the meal of roast goose, boar's head, brawn, and mincemeat pies, Mama tapped her lips with her serviette. "It is my dearest apology that we do not have a pudding to serve. Due to a mistake in the kitchens late at night, my scrumptious plum pudding which had been aging for weeks was, well, it was destroyed."

Selina covered her own mouth with her serviette, her eyes darting across the table to Edmund. His lips twisted with a smile, the first she had seen from him all night. Warmth spread through her bones and she sat back in her chair. A chorus of dismay passed over the group.

"How was it destroyed?" Mrs. Godwin asked, her eyes round.

Mama glanced at Edmund before shaking her head. "I haven't the slightest idea. Not to worry. A new pudding has been stirred up and will be served at our Twelfth Night party. I expect you have already received my invitations? You must taste it. In fact, it was my own daughter and our guest Sir Edmund who prepared it. It is all part of the enjoyment of the holidays."

Mrs. Godwin seemed surprised by that, but said nothing more, taking a sip from her goblet.

Selina exchanged another glance with Edmund, no longer hiding her smile. Once he left, she would never think of plum pudding in the same way. She could never smell it or eat it without thinking of him. The idea sent a surge of grief through her chest. Not the pudding, but the leaving.

When the meal was over, Rose turned to Mama with a voice loud enough to carry over the entire table. "My legs are quite stiff from so many hours in a carriage. I would very much like to dance."

Mama's eyebrows rose. "I have not prepared a room for dancing."

"Well, send the servants at once," Rose said. "It will not take long, and I am certain your guests would enjoy a little frivolity this evening."

Declarations of assent came from the Godwins and the Setons.

Mama did not usually enjoy straying from her plans, but for Rose, she would do anything. "Then a dance we shall have."

CHAPTER 15

L ess than an hour had passed before the servants had successfully emptied a room in the house, even bringing a pianoforte into the corner where Mrs. Ellis had volunteered to play the music. Edmund surveyed the undecorated, dimly lit room. His footsteps echoed in the empty space, and the quiet of the room reminded him of how quiet the library had been earlier that day with Selina.

He had come far too close to kissing her. He had been scolding himself all day, reliving the moment through his mind repeatedly. What had come over him? He would have been such a fool to kiss her when she was still engaged to Skinner, and while he was staying as a guest in the same household. Thankfully, his better judgement had gained control over his desires in time. But only just.

When he reached the center of the room, he turned around, watching as Rose and her husband walked through the doors, followed by Selina and the other guests. Mr. and Mrs. Godwin had one daughter and a son, and the Setons had one daughter in attendance. With an extra lady in attendance, Edmund would likely have to dance each set. But he hoped Selina would be his first partner.

She stood with her hands clasped together, surveying the room nervously.

He approached her, smiling in an attempt to pull the same expression from her serious face. She had been doing that often —alternating between expressions as if she did not know whether she was displeased or happy with Edmund's company. She was shy one moment and teasing him the next. He could only hope that the cause of it all was that she cared for him more than she believed she ought.

"Your mother failed to mention several important details regarding the pudding incident," Edmund said in a secretive voice as he stopped by Selina's side.

As he had hoped, a smile curved her lips. "And there are still several details she does not know of." Selina shot him a quick glance. "Such as the fact that you are not to blame at all."

"I did give you enough of a fright to make you drop the pudding when I opened the door."

"That is true. But my plan was to leave it on the floor outside your room in a similar state. The only difference was that I didn't think I would be caught."

Edmund tipped his head back with a chuckle. He preferred Selina this way, when she could laugh with him and speak of lighter things. But he also liked that he could speak of serious matters with her just as easily. The only subject that seemed to cause conflict between them was Mr. Noah Skinner. And Edmund would cause conflict with *him* if he ever hurt Selina. It was impossible to know for certain all that was happening in Selina's guarded heart, but he did know for certain what was happening in his.

He was falling in love with her.

Devil take it, *he was*, and there was nothing he could do about it.

"May I have the honor of your first two dances, Miss Selina Ellis?" Edmund moved to face her fully, lowering his head in a bow before raising his gaze to hers.

She seemed surprised, despite the fact that there were only a few couples in the empty room. His smile grew as the shock melted off her face, replaced with the nonchalant look he had come to know so well. "Yes," she said, her curls bouncing with the nod that accompanied the word. "It is an honor, indeed."

He raised one eyebrow, mouthing the word *pompous* just as Rose approached from behind him. Selina hid her smile.

"Shall we waltz?" Rose asked.

Edmund nodded, and Selina did the same. Whether the German or the French, the waltz was a much more intimate dance than others like the quadrille or scotch reel. The partners were required to be closer, with a greater focus on one another than the others dancing alongside them.

"It will not be the same without violins," Mrs. Ellis called from behind the pianoforte, "but I will play to the best of my ability."

From the corner of his eye, Edmund saw Mr. Vaughan escort Rose to the center of the floor, as well as the other pairings. Edmund turned to Selina, extending his hand to her. She placed her gloved fingers lightly over his, her smile fading into a look of concentration as he led her closer to the other couples who had begun lining up.

When they reached the center of the floor, Edmund turned to face Selina, keeping hold of her hand and placing his other hand at her waist, wrapping it around to her back, holding her close. With Mrs. Ellis, Rose, and her husband to see it, he would have no qualms about holding Selina so closely—even closer than the dance demanded—while he could. They likely wished he would hold her closer.

Selina's chest rose and fell with a deep breath as her gaze flitted to her sister and Mr. Vaughan. Edmund tipped his head down in order to draw her eyes to him, his heart flipping in an unnatural way when her gaze met his. He swallowed, bringing a slight smile to his lips. Why did he feel just as bashful as she appeared? He had danced the waltz with other women but dancing it with Selina was different. His lungs protested for air as the music began.

Selina's fingers tightened on his, and he pressed her closer to him. How could he be graceful when he was feeling so weak? His concentration on the steps faltered more than once as they turned in time with the music. Mrs. Ellis played the song much slower than it was meant to be played, giving Edmund more time to keep Selina close before releasing her waist as the steps demanded, bringing her back to him between each motion. Selina's gaze trapped him. If she told him she could read his thoughts, he would believe her.

The golden curls on her brow reminded him of the ribbons they had sorted, the intensity of her eyes reminding him of the way she had examined him while they played chess. She was searching for something in his eyes, just as he was searching hers.

This time, she wasn't looking for proof of his next move on the chessboard. He had done all he could to hide that proof from her; but tonight, he had every intention of proving something far more important.

When the last note rang out from the pianoforte, Selina stumbled a little, finding her balance as he steadied her waist. She stared at his waistcoat before glancing up at him from beneath her lashes, slowly tearing her gaze away. They both turned toward Mrs. Ellis, who stood from the pianoforte. Her curtsy demanded applause, so Edmund released his hold on Selina. His smile had faded during their dance, and finding it again was difficult.

How could he tell her to leave Skinner behind? She did not even know of her inheritance yet. Skinner had told him she would learn of it with the new year. Edmund promised himself that if she had not already made the decision not to marry Skinner by then, he would tell her the man's intentions himself. Nothing hurt him more than the thought of Selina married to Skinner. Not even the loss of his grandmother's inheritance. How could he trade possessions for Selina's happiness?

Edmund would continue to tread carefully, at least while he was still unsure of her feelings. Her trust was won little by little, and so he would continue being her friend.

After three more dances and switching partners between them, the group removed to the drawing room where Rose sang and played the pianoforte. Edmund preferred Christmas festivities with such a small gathering of people, especially since it meant Selina could remain by his side.

Just before they retired for the evening, Selina glanced at

Edmund from her place beside him on the sofa, a smile pulling on her lips. "Happy Christmas."

Warmth ignited in his chest, and when he spoke, his voice came out weak. "Happy Christmas."

❄

The next day, Edmund challenged Selina to a third match of chess, and it quickly became a daily tradition. Selina could hardly remember a year when the space between Christmas day and New Year's Eve had passed so quickly. With Rose and her husband staying at the house, the days were filled with games, desserts, and discussions by the fireplace. Between it all, Selina's favorite moments were when she and Edmund played chess or walked together from one room to the next, always greeted with sly smiles from Mama and Rose. Selina's stomach had tied itself in knots on more than one occasion as she thought of how different their expressions would be if they knew it wasn't Edmund she had promised her heart to.

She hadn't seen Noah since Christmas Day, but he had told her to meet him the morning of New Year's Eve. Each time she thought of the preparations he must have been making for their elopement, dread flooded her chest. She would have to tell him to put an end to it. She would have to break his heart.

But as she examined her feelings, she realized that her heart would be left whole, if not a bit better than it was before, once she finally bid Noah farewell for good. She hadn't missed him in the days since they had last spoken. She had hardly thought of him. The anxiety the entire situation had caused would soon be over. A pang of guilt struck her. Disappointing him would be the hardest thing she had ever done.

Her anxiety rose each time she considered what she would say to Edmund. Was her attachment to Noah the only thing keeping him from declaring his feelings for her? The idea made her heart pound, and she didn't dare dwell on it for long. How disappointed *she* would be if it wasn't true.

With Rose visiting, Mama insisted that they take yet another trip to the Frost Fair before the ice could have a chance to melt. So on the day before New Year's Eve, they paid the excessive price to set foot on the River Thames one last time. Rose was every bit as fascinated with it as Selina had been on her first visit, and Selina wondered if she had imagined the ill feelings she had held toward her sister. It wasn't Rose's fault she had been favored. And now, with her visits so rare, it was natural for Mama to dote on her. Selina smiled as the three of them walked across the ice, arm in arm. She glanced over her shoulder, finding no sign of Edmund.

He remained out of sight for much of their time at the fair, until he finally reappeared as they were preparing to leave, his arms wrapped tightly around his coat.

"Where have you been?" Selina asked. And why was he holding his coat so strangely? She raised one eyebrow.

Edmund shifted on his feet. "I lost my way." Without another word, he strode forward, following behind the others in their group. As if remembering something important, he turned back, nearly slipping as he offered Selina his arm. Even as he escorted her off the ice, he still held his coat carefully. She gave a curious smile, studying the side of his face. His mouth was serious, his eyes fixed straight ahead. She said nothing, keeping a close eye on his coat to see if it might reveal what he was hiding.

"Did you enjoy your visit to the fair?" she asked.

Edmund nodded. "It was equally diverting as the last two visits." He cast her a lopsided smile. "Well, perhaps not so much so as the first one."

Since he mentioned it, Selina watched the ice, careful to avoid falling on him again. Her curiosity continued to rise as she watched him adjust a small lump under his coat.

"You did not lose your way today, did you, Edmund?" she blurted.

He looked at her with wide eyes, seemingly shocked by her sudden accusation. "I did, indeed."

"I suspect you were buying yourself a souvenir, despite your determination not to bend to the steep prices the fair demands." She cast him a sneaky smile. "There is no need to hide your treasure from me. Tell me what you found that you could not resist." She cast a pointed look at his coat.

Edmund held her gaze for several seconds, maintaining his innocent, round eyes. The expression reminded Selina of when he was a child, and she nearly burst out laughing. "Not to worry. I will not reveal your secret to anyone. You have my *silence*." She kept her voice quiet so Mama would not overhear.

"It is nothing," Edmund said, his voice much less amused than she had expected it to be. Was he offended by her teasing? She clamped her mouth shut.

"Won't you tell me what it is?"

He shook his head, avoiding her gaze.

Her heart plummeted as Edmund handed her inside the coach without another word, crossing his arms tightly around himself once more. Selina looked out the window as they drove home, her brow furrowed. She had never seen Edmund so . . . odd. By the time they reached home without a word passed between them, Selina was certain she had done something to offend him.

Even at dinner, he retired early to his room with a simple, "Goodnight."

Selina's heart stung as she climbed the stairs, an ache spreading through her limbs. Perhaps she had been wrong about everything, not only about Noah. Perhaps she had also been wrong to believe that Edmund cared for her at all. He was a polite, amiable gentleman, who treated every lady with respect. The image of Edmund and Miss Perry beneath the kissing bough flitted through her mind again, and she banished it at once, fighting against the uncertainty that swirled in her heart. Until she was no longer engaged to Noah, Edmund had every reason to be distant, she reassured herself. Tomorrow when she saw Noah, everything would change. But her entire body still ached with disappointment as she walked around the last corner to her bedchamber.

She stopped in the hall, catching sight of a small brown package wrapped in a gold ribbon, placed just outside her door.

Glancing to each side, she found the hall deserted. Placed where it was, the package could only have been for her. Her heart pounded as she bent down to retrieve it, slipping inside her room before tugging on one end of the ribbon. It unraveled, and the brown paper spread open.

She pressed one hand to her chest. The miniature tiger statue she had admired her first day at the fair sat atop the paper, one paw lifted as if to strike. She traced her finger over the engraved stripes, and her other hand crept to her throat as it tightened with emotion. Had Edmund done this?

Who else could it have been?

She scoured the packaging for a note but found nothing. It was improper for Edmund to give Selina a gift, even during Christmastide. The exchanging of gifts was never condoned among single men and women, so Edmund had not signed his name on the gift, knowing it would still be recognized as his.

Her heart thudded as a tear escaped the corner of her eye. She had been worried for nothing. Edmund had been thinking of her the entire fair, and the rest of the day that followed. He had not been aloof. He had only been vexed that she had nearly ruined his surprise.

She sniffed, scooping up the tiger and placing it on her writing desk. Tomorrow she would thank him. Tomorrow all would be made right.

And she was fairly certain that, despite her worry over facing Mr. Skinner, she would sleep with a smile plastered on her face.

CHAPTER 16

❄

Selina ate breakfast alone the morning of New Year's Eve, waiting a little longer than usual in her chair to see if Edmund would come to the breakfast room. She had spent the night searching for the right words to thank him for his thoughtful gift but hadn't been able to find ones that would adequately explain what it meant to her. What *he* meant to her.

There was no proper way for her to tell him the latter—at least not until he confessed similar feelings to her. And certainly not until she broke her engagement with Noah.

She had told Noah she would come by his father's office in the morning, but they had not planned a specific time. She scraped the prongs of her fork across her plate, dreading the moment she would have to speak the *other* words she had been practicing.

As she mulled through all that weighed on her mind, the door creaked open. Selina glanced up quickly, a broad smile on her face. But it wasn't Edmund at the door. Mama stood in her white morning dress, hands clasped in front of her.

"Good morning, Selina."

"Good morning, Mama." Selina eyed her carefully. What was that eager smile all about?

"There is a secret I have been keeping from you," Mama said, her smile growing. "And I wish to tell you as my New Year's gift to you."

Selina frowned. How many gifts could she be given in such a short time? She studied Mama's expression, relieved to find that she seemed quite happy with this secret. The worry faded from Selina's chest, allowing her lungs to fill with air. She hadn't realized that she had been holding her breath. "I did not know you were one to keep secrets."

Mama laughed. "Well, this one was far too delicate to share until now."

"Are you marrying again?" Selina guessed.

"Oh, heavens no!" Mama threw out her hand. "But this secret of mine . . . it could make it far easier for *you* to marry well."

Selina's confusion increased more with each passing second.

"Come with me," Mama said. "We will be more comfortable in the drawing room."

Selina's brow furrowed as she followed Mama into the hallway, and she jumped a little when Mama closed the drawing room door behind them.

"Now that we are in a more private place," Mama said, "I may tell you."

Selina's heart pounded as she waited for the revelation of Mama's strange secret.

Mama took a deep breath before walking forward to take Selina's hands. "You are a very wealthy young woman."

Selina raised both eyebrows. "Pardon me?"

"Do you remember your Aunt and Uncle Ellis in Cheshire? Well, Mr. Ellis has made a fortune in his trade. With no children of their own, Mr. Ellis thought to give a portion to his late brother's daughter, and another portion to me." Mama's eyes filled with tears. "His generosity has left you with a portion amounting to roughly fifteen thousand pounds."

Selina's jaw dropped, and she covered her mouth with one hand. "Fifteen thousand?"

Mama gave her arm a tight squeeze. "Indeed. Can you even believe it?"

Selina's head spun. That must have been why Mama had taken the liberties she had with hosting so many dinner parties and purchasing new decorations. She had been given money too, enough to support her for years to come. "When did you learn of this?" Selina asked, her voice still tight with shock. "How long have you kept it from me?"

"There were many arrangements I had to make with the solicitor several months ago, before it could all be made final." Mama's eyes glistened. "Think of how much more eager Sir Edmund will be to marry you when he discovers your inheritance."

Selina's stomach dropped. "I don't think Edmund would be influenced too greatly by money."

Mama laughed, swatting her hand through the air. "Any man would."

Selina scowled at the ground as she tried to slow her racing thoughts, struggling to grasp onto just one at a time.

"What a wonderful new year this will be," Mama said. "To usher it in with good fortune such as this? I expect we shall be reaping our rewards of good fortune all year long."

Selina looked up, putting a smile on her face. "I thank you for telling me today. It is a much better gift than I could have ever asked for."

Mama nodded. "Nothing could compare."

As they discussed a few more of the details of her inheritance, Selina hardly heard a thing. She stared out the drawing room window, watching the light snowfall as if it held the answers she sought.

Any man would.

Her thoughts traveled back to her conversation with Edmund by the fire in the library on Christmas Day, when he had asked her if Noah had ever told her *why* he wished to marry her. She had not known the answer then, but a suspicion had begun creeping into her mind, driving a sharp pain into her heart.

Had he never loved her at all?

Could he have known of her inheritance from the beginning?

When they made their way back into the hallway, Selina walked slowly back toward her room, trying to stop her legs from shaking. When she took the first three steps up the staircase, Edmund appeared at the top, starting down the stairs toward her.

She steadied her hand on the banister, watching Edmund's boots as he approached. When he stopped just two stairs above her, she looked up. His concerned expression brought a lump to her throat. "Edmund." She shook her head. "I have just received the most unexpected news." She was still struggling to believe that it was true. "I cannot comprehend it, even now, after nearly an hour has passed since I heard it."

Edmund did not seem surprised at all, his features flickering with understanding. "Your inheritance."

Selina's eyes rounded. "You knew? How did you learn of this before I did?"

He gave a slow nod, his jaw tight, as if he regretted making her aware of his knowledge. "I cannot tell you that. Not yet. But I must ask that you trust me."

Selina's heart thudded as she was reminded of her mother's words. *Any* man would be enticed by money. Could that mean Edmund was too? If he had already known of her inheritance, then that could have been the reason he was seeking to win her affections during his visit. She recalled how determined he had been to keep her away from Noah when he had first come to London. Was it because he wanted her fortune for himself? Mama's secret had obviously not been as well-kept as she thought it had.

Dread settled heavily into her stomach.

"Why did you suddenly wish to spend time with me?" Selina asked.

Edmund's brow furrowed. "What do you mean?"

"We seemed to be rivals until one day you began treating me differently." She took a deep breath, asking the question that burned in her throat. "You seemed as though you were determined to win my affections. Was it because you hoped to win my fortune?"

"No." Edmund stepped down a stair, bending down to look at her face. "That was never the reason."

"Then what was the reason?" Selina fought the tears

burning behind her eyes. She had to know if Edmund cared for her or not. No matter the answer, she had to know. She fixed him with a stern look, not allowing him to lie or escape her question.

Edmund released a slow breath. "When my efforts to separate you from Skinner failed, I decided that in order to help you realize that you did not care for him as you thought, I would encourage you to . . . fall in love with me instead. I thought you might learn that what you felt for Skinner was not any stronger than what you could feel for me." He regarded her seriously, his brows drawing together. "That was how it began, but I assure you, I feel differently now."

Selina blinked hard, her heart pounding. She backed away one step, then another, until her feet hit the base of the stairs. Betrayal stung in her chest. "If you did not want my fortune, then why did you think to toy with my heart in such a way in order to keep me from Mr. Skinner? How do I know if you have been lying about him all this time? Perhaps you were the one deceiving me, not him." A tear hovered on her lashes, falling slowly down her cheek.

Edmund moved to the base of the stairs to stand in front of her, swiping away the tear on her cheek with his thumb. He opened his mouth to speak before his gaze lifted to the window behind her, his eyes narrowing slightly. She turned, following his gaze to where Noah stood in the snow just behind the house. Her heart leaped. "What is he doing here?"

She cast one more look at Edmund before hurrying to the door. She had to stop Noah before Mama could see him. Her mind still spun with questions as she stepped out into the frigid air, wrapping her arms around herself. She hadn't stopped to put on her coat, so a shiver had already begun its ascent over her skin.

"Selina." Noah walked toward her, leaving deep prints in the snow. "I was very worried when you didn't come."

As he approached, her stomach tightened in a knot. His face showed genuine concern, but she couldn't help but wonder if it was for her . . . or her fifteen thousand pounds. His hands wrapped around hers as he reached her, just as they always did, but today they were cold.

"What delayed you?" he asked, his intense brown eyes boring into hers.

"My mother had some unexpected news to relay to me. I am still in awe when I think of it." Selina shivered again.

Noah's eyes sparked with interest. "What did she tell you?"

"Of my inheritance."

"Inheritance?" Noah's voice rose with surprise, though her insides remained unsettled.

"Did you know I was inheriting fifteen thousand pounds?" Selina held his gaze as firmly as she could.

Noah shook his head fast. "I hadn't the slightest idea, but that is astonishing news, indeed." He gave a broad smile. "How did I manage to be so fortunate as to marry a woman of such beauty and fortune? Though, as you already know, I would marry you no matter your financial situation." He gazed into her eyes, but he failed to look half as genuine as Edmund had moments before.

What had Edmund been about to say to her? When he had seen Noah out the window, his words had been stopped short. He had told her he had begun by trying to secure her affections without intending to fall in love with her, but that he felt differently now. Her heart pounded. But how could he explain how he knew of her inheritance?

Noah's voice pulled her thoughts back to him. "Is something amiss?"

She shifted uncomfortably; snow had begun melting through her sleeves. Had his grip on her hands tightened? She couldn't be certain. Before she could lose her courage, she took a deep breath. "Yes."

"What is it, my love?"

His words would have melted her heart once, but now they felt very much like a lie. "I cannot marry you."

The concern melted off his brow, his eyes flashing with shock. "I'm afraid I don't understand. What has caused this hesitation?" The tone of his voice grew harder.

"I have been hesitant all along," Selina said, keeping her voice confident. "I—I did not have the courage to tell you."

The roundness of Noah's eyes flattened slightly, his jaw tightening. "Was this Sir Edmund's doing? What has he told you?"

Selina's heart sprung against her chest, and she was tempted to tug her hands from his grip. She had obeyed Edmund's request not to mention his presence at her home, or not to mention his name at all. So why had Noah suspected him to be responsible for her doubts? She maintained an innocent expression. "Sir Edmund? I have not seen him since that day at the Frost Fair."

Noah studied her face with no small amount of skepticism but didn't question her further. She exhaled slowly to calm her racing heart.

"Well, there is no reason for you to hesitate. We have agreed to marry, and so we shall. All the arrangements have been made."

He smiled down at her as if nothing had changed, as if her refusal meant nothing.

She shook her head. "I meant what I said. I will not marry you."

He laughed under his breath, glancing heavenward before meeting her gaze again. "There is no need for that."

"I don't want to marry you." She spoke each word firmly so he would not misunderstand.

"You do not know what you want, Selina. You are nervous, that is all." Noah's voice was final, and his hands tightened around hers. Her pulse pounded past her ears as panic spread through her veins. Where was Edmund? Her back was to the house, so he couldn't see that she was distressed.

Noah leaned closer, and before she could glance back at the house, he pressed his lips firmly to hers, holding the back of her neck so she couldn't pull away as quickly as she wanted to. Her body froze with shock until she fully realized what was happening. Her mind snapped to attention, and she pulled away, but he brought her lips back to his forcefully. He still gripped her right hand, but she used her left to push against him, sending him staggering back a pace. Her face was hot with anger. She tried to wrench her other hand free, but his grip was firm.

She had imagined many times what it might be like to kiss him—how sweet and romantic it would be—but in reality, his kiss both frightened and disgusted her.

He took a step forward and stroked her hair, tracing his fingers down the side of her face. "Think of all you will miss if you refuse to marry me."

A shiver of revulsion stiffened her muscles, and all she could think was how she wished Edmund were here to help her. It was clear to her now that Noah had been the one toying with her all this time. Edmund had warned her, but she had been too stubborn to listen. Too prideful and blind.

"Let me go." She glared up at Noah. "You will never have my money. And you will never have me." In one swift motion, she jerked her arm away from him, running back toward the house. Her lungs burned from the cold air, and the moment she was safely inside, tears carved a path of warmth down her cheeks. She drew a shaking breath, wiping her lips with her sleeve to rid them of the taste of Noah's kiss. Where was Edmund? She had to apologize for her lack of trust in him. He had been right about everything. She hadn't even thanked him for his gift the night before.

Her gaze darted to the staircase, but he was gone.

※

Edmund had never understood a woman so clearly until today. When Selina had rushed away to her room after seeing Miss Perry kiss him, he had been surprised by her actions. He had been certain jealousy would never bring him to do such a thing.

But here he was behind the doors of the library, where he had marched off to hide the moment he saw Selina kiss Skinner. Seeing their passionate embrace from the window had shattered a glass inside him, and the shards had cut deep.

His chest rose and fell with quickened breath, a deep ache spreading through his chest. As much as he had hoped that she no longer cared for Skinner, he was wrong. No matter what Edmund did, he would always be second in Selina's affections. He had been sure she felt *something* for him, but he could have imagined it all. After seeing her in Skinner's arms, and hearing her accusations toward himself today, he felt very close to giving up.

There was no way he could prove that he wasn't seeking her money, but he had thought he had gained enough of her trust that she would believe him to be innocent. And if Edmund had stopped Selina from going outside to meet Skinner—or if he had accompanied her—then Skinner would have burned the will that very day.

Edmund had suspected Selina meant to break off her engagement with Skinner, but their conversation had obviously not ended in such a way.

His jaw tightened as he fought against the image of Selina in Skinner's arms. He scuffed his boot across the floor, crossing his arms over his chest. If she would be so careless as to kiss the man outside of her house, then he could not stop her from marrying him. A sharp pain dug into his heart, and he pushed it away. He had given her too much credit. She was too naive to be helped.

He could still tell her the truth. Even if she would not believe him when he did. Then the decision would be hers, and Edmund could stay out of it. Though, even if she chose not to marry Skinner, it did not mean she would marry Edmund. He was a friend to her, nothing more, and it was his own fault his heart had become so invested.

"Edmund?"

His arms stiffened at the sound of Selina's muffled voice. She seemed to be walking the hallway in search of him. Before he could move, the library doors opened, and Selina's round eyes shot up to his. The moment he saw her face, his defenses rose, and he crossed his arms tighter.

"Edmund," she breathed as if relieved to see him. "What are you doing in here?"

His visceral, defensive reaction had thrown walls up around his heart in a matter of mere minutes. They constricted his lungs, making it difficult to breathe.

"Have you been in here for long?" she asked when he didn't answer. She stared up at him nervously, clearly hoping he hadn't witnessed what had just occurred outside.

He kept his arms crossed, watching the ground as he spoke. "Do not concern yourself with me."

"You have concerned yourself with me many times." Her voice shook. "I meant to thank you for the gift. It—it was the best thing anyone has ever given me."

"You seemed to enjoy Skinner's offering even more just now." Edmund immediately regretted the force of his voice.

Selina's eyes widened before her brow furrowed into a scowl. "Do you think I encouraged him to kiss me?" Her voice rose in defense. "That kiss was . . . it was completely unbidden."

Edmund returned his gaze to the floor. A man would not need encouragement to kiss Selina. His frustration rose. "I expect it is not the first time he has kissed you, and it may not even be the last. You may do as you wish with him if you cannot trust me enough to believe my warnings concerning him." She had accused Edmund of seeking her fortune, but had she even considered Skinner to be doing the same? She was so blind. "He has only courted you all this time for your fortune. He does not love you, and he never has. I discovered this shortly after coming into town, and he threatened to burn my grandmother's will if I told you a word of it. That is why I have done all I could to keep you from him while still keeping his secret and yours. Perhaps now you will believe me."

Selina pressed a hand to her chest. "Your grandmother's will?"

"Yes." Edmund swallowed. "But since you still obviously intend to marry him, it seems the will is safe." Without looking at her face, he lowered his head, walking past her. "Good day," he said as he opened the door and disappeared into the hallway.

Frustration coursed through him as he took two steps away, then stopped. Had there been tears in her eyes? He hadn't looked closely enough. Regret seeped through the walls around his heart, and he nearly walked back into the library. Had he been the one to cause her to cry?

He glanced back once before forcing himself to walk forward. He had done all he could. Perhaps it was best that his hope be gone forever.

As he strode toward the banister, he stopped when he noticed Skinner still outside the window, but much closer now. Edmund didn't have time to move out of sight. Skinner's eyes fell on Edmund through the glass. A flash of anger passed over his face, followed by realization.

He kicked at the snow, sending a cloud of it into the air before storming in the opposite direction.

Edmund watched him go, his brow furrowing. If Skinner still had Selina, then why was he so upset?

"I told him I would not marry him." Selina's firm voice came from behind Edmund.

He turned to face her, heart pounding. A mixture of relief and dread flooded his chest. "When?"

"Just before he tried to convince me otherwise by kissing me without my consent." Her eyes flashed. "You did not let me explain." Without another word, she turned on her heel, marching toward the staircase as she always did.

Shame burned on his skin. He had reacted poorly, to be sure. He had reacted like a child. He groaned, turning back toward the window. His mind raced. Skinner had just seen Edmund through the window . . . *after* Selina had broken their engagement. Who else would Skinner blame?

Dread sank further into his stomach. Skinner would be taking his revenge as soon as he returned to his office.

Edmund threw a glance up the stairs. Selina must have already reached the top, likely tucked away in her room. His heart ached, and he wanted to mend their misunderstandings, but for now, he had to save what was most pressing. He couldn't let Skinner betray Selina's heart and his grandmother's wishes all in one day.

With a deep breath, he pulled open the door and strode out into the snow.

CHAPTER 17

❄

*D*espite her fifteen thousand pounds, Selina felt very
much without good fortune as New Year's Day came
and went. Edmund had disappeared for most of the previous
afternoon and had seemed to be avoiding her ever since. The
friendship they had built seemed to have vanished, replaced with
fleeting glances that always ended in either Selina or Edmund
looking away. She couldn't help but wonder if Edmund had
confronted Noah the day before and if that had been why he had
been gone for so long. She had been worried all evening that
they had dueled or done something far more drastic than the
situation demanded. Was Edmund's inheritance safe? She had
been meaning to ask him, but she was afraid to hear the answer.
By the way he avoided her, she could only guess that he held her
responsible for whatever had happened.

She had known she would feel free after turning Noah away,
but without Edmund as her friend, she didn't even care. If
Edmund's sole purpose in spending time with her had been to

drive her away from Noah, then he had accomplished his purpose. And now he was clearly through with her.

Each time Selina passed Edmund, his brow was furrowed into a distinct scowl, leading her to believe he was just as troubled and confused as she was. Mama had questioned him more than once on his serious state, but he had failed to give a plausible answer. Selina had thought she had been hiding her distress well until Mama found her in the drawing room the next afternoon.

Selina sat by the window, watching as yet another snowstorm swirled from the sky. Alone as she was, she had allowed a few tears to slip from her eyes, wiping at them with the heel of her hand.

Mama came through the doors without warning, and Selina didn't turn her face toward the window quickly enough.

"Selina! You must tell me what the matter is." Mama marched into the room. "I was fully expecting an engagement to occur between you and Sir Edmund and now the two of you will hardly spare a glance toward one another." Mama let out a flustered breath. "And you are crying alone by the window. That always means there is something quite distressing on your mind. What did you do to dissuade Sir Edmund's affections?"

Selina swallowed, shaking her head. "I doubt I ever had his affections." She wiped at another stray tear. "And if I did have them, they are gone forever. I have made several mistakes, and I have not trusted him as I ought to have. At the moment, we do not understand one another."

Mama was silent for a long moment, her blue eyes narrowing as she studied Selina's face. "Well, you must speak with him until you do understand. Surely a conversation could sort through it all."

"He does not wish to see me." Selina let out a long breath. "He does not care for me anymore. I have ruined his life by being so naive and stubborn." She sniffed. "It does not seem fair that I have my fortune, one I do not even deserve, and he has lost the inheritance from his dear grandmother because of me."

"What do you mean?" Mama's eyebrows shot upward.

Selina wrapped her arms around herself, crossing her ankles beneath her chair. "That is a tale for another time, Mama. It will take too long to explain." She didn't want to speak of or even think of Noah anymore. He was vile and cruel, and she had thought herself to be in love with him. It was embarrassing to think of how witless Edmund must have assumed her to be. Fresh tears escaped her eyes, rolling down her cheeks.

Mama let out a sigh as if frustrated to be kept in the dark but accepting of it, nonetheless. To Selina's surprise, Mama wrapped her arms around her, pulling Selina's head down to her shoulder. "You cannot pretend to be indifferent to him now." She said in a firm voice. "I have never seen you cry like this."

Selina shook her head against Mama's shoulder. She couldn't remember the last time Mama had held her like this, and the comfort it brought was enough to make her cry even more. "I have cried like this before, but never for you to see." Selina pressed her lips together. "I cried when I heard you tell your sister that your life would have been much better if I had not been born as your daughter. You told her that you prayed for a son and that you were disappointed the first time you held me." Selina sniffed, calming her shaking voice. "You told her that you set me in the nursery and hired a wet nurse so you would not have to hold me for weeks. As a child, I had wondered why you favored Rose, and when I heard your conversation with your sister, I finally understood. I was not able to be an heir and save Papa's estate. Because of me, you lost the prestige you had married him for."

Mama's arm had stiffened, and Selina stared out the window, shocked with herself for even speaking those things aloud. She had kept them in her heart throughout her entire childhood, and they had been festering far too long. What other feelings would she speak aloud if she wasn't careful? Perhaps it was best that Edmund wasn't speaking to her of late.

Mama's shoulder began wriggling as if to force Selina to lift her head. The moment Selina did, Mama took Selina's face between her hands, wiping away her tears. "Oh, my dear Selina." Mama's own eyes glistened with moisture. "Have you truly felt this way for so long? I—I did not mean to give you the indication that—" she paused, collecting her thoughts. "I love you and Rose equally. I should never have made you feel otherwise, and for that, I am most sorry. It was never my intention. I confess I used to think that your birth meant I was not worthy of a miracle, but now I see that you were a miracle. If I had been given what I wanted—a son—I would not have you. I would not be here in London, a place I have come to love so much. My life would be so different, and so inferior without you in it. What I wanted and what I needed were two different things."

Selina's heart pounded as she recognized those words. Edmund had told her the same thing.

Mama brushed back the curls on Selina's brow. "Can you ever forgive me for those things you overheard? I was upset and confused for many years, but I have always loved you. I do not want anything about my life or your life to be different." She paused. "Well, perhaps I would wish for you to marry Sir Edmund, but only if you would be happy."

Selina smiled, rubbing her nose. "I do forgive you." With those words, Selina's entire body felt lighter. Her heart still ached with uncertainty toward Edmund, but she had her mother on her side. For the first time in her life, she felt a strong alliance between them as well as a familial bond. Mama wanted the same thing Selina did.

"And yes. I would be very happy with Edmund," Selina whispered. It was the first time she had admitted that to herself, and it filled her chest with warmth. "But I fear I have driven him away forever. I cannot make amends if he will not even speak to me."

A slow smile of determination dawned on Mama's face. "You may leave that to me."

CHAPTER 18

$\mathcal{E}$dmund watched the front of his boots as they displaced small piles of snow. He hadn't been able to think clearly enough inside the warm house, so he had taken what he had intended to be a short walk, hoping the cold air would clear his mind. By the numbness in his hands and feet, he could assume he had been outside for much longer than a few minutes. The sun had begun descending, leaving the sky a dull grey. The snow had stopped falling, thankfully, but that didn't make him any less cold.

And the cold didn't make him any less confused.

In his attempt to confront Skinner the day before, Edmund had been unable to find him at his father's office. The same clerk who had greeted Edmund on his first visit to the solicitor's office had still been unwilling to answer the specific questions Edmund had, but he had given Edmund a slight suspicion.

Skinner, an expert in manipulation, might have fooled Edmund as well.

The clerk had been brief in what he shared, but the conversation had been replaying in Edmund's mind all day.

"Who is your grandmother?" The clerk had asked.

"Mrs. Frederica Sharp."

The clerk had disappeared for a few minutes before returning, deep creases in his aged brow. "According to my records, Mrs. Sharp neglected to entrust the will to Mr. Skinner. However, before his journey took him away from the office, Mrs. Sharp did sign the will with witnesses, but she claimed to have plans to leave the will in her grandson's possession." The clerk's eyes had risen to examine Edmund. "Are you this grandson she speaks of?"

Edmund had considered that the clerk could have simply been confused, but then the possibility that Skinner had been lying seemed to make much more sense.

Skinner reveled in deceiving people, and he had needed a way to keep Edmund silent. When he had heard Edmund speaking of his grandmother's will that first day in the office, he must have pretended to hold it above the flames when it had been a different document entirely.

As he struggled to remember every detail of that day, Edmund realized he never had seen the front of the document. He had been just as easily fooled as Selina.

But then where was the will?

Edmund tucked his hands under his arms to keep them warm as he made his way back from his second search of his grandmother's house. He had looked through every cabinet and drawer, every stack in the study. He had spoken to her servants, who also hadn't heard of the whereabouts. If she had been so ill and had realized Edmund would likely not make it there before her death, why hadn't she told one of her servants where the will was kept? She had been very slow to trust anyone, but she had always trusted Edmund. He liked to think she was a good judge of character, and that was why she hadn't left the will at the office with the younger Mr. Skinner.

His initial relief had turned to frustration as he realized he might never find it. How much better was a missing will than a burned one?

He stopped when he reached the house, pausing outside to look up to the first window on the second floor. With the fading daylight, he could see the faint glow of candlelight from inside.

Was Selina in her room? She had spent much of the last two days upstairs, and he had been away for too long to inquire after her. And he was embarrassed to face her after all he had misunderstood about her kiss with Skinner. She had needed him, and he had been too selfish and envious to help her. He had been just as accusatory and unwilling to listen to her as she had once been to him. All he wanted was to be her friend again. If she was willing, perhaps they might grow to be something more. He would not blame her if she didn't trust him immediately after the betrayal she had endured from Skinner. But he would be patient; he would love her for as long as she let him.

He let out a shaky breath. His heart thudded as the light extinguished from her window. It must be time for dinner.

❄

Mama did not tell Selina what her plan entailed, and Selina was glad of it. She would rather not know what schemes Mama had in mind to find a way for Edmund to be alone with her. With a deep breath, she smoothed out the light wrinkles in her skirts, blowing out the candles in her room before heading downstairs for dinner.

She hadn't heard Edmund come home yet. He hadn't told her or Mama where he had disappeared to for the second day in a row. But just as she reached the base of the stairs, Edmund walked through the front doors, bringing a gust of cold air with him. He removed his hat, revealing more of his face, which was slightly pink from the cold.

She stopped, her heart leaping when he looked across the entry hall at her. How long had he been outside? She could still feel a chill in the air as though he had absorbed enough of the cold to bring it inside with him. "Where have you been, Edmund?" Selina asked in a quiet voice. She held the base of the banister with her gloved hand, hoping it would steady her.

He removed his coat and gloves, walking slowly toward the place she stood. "I have had business to attend to." He gave a weak smile as his blue eyes roamed her face. Silence fell between them for several seconds. She wished he would smile the way he used to. He had been far too serious of late. But at least he was speaking to her. She tried to focus on that positive thought as she glanced down the hall behind him.

Mama was incapable of making a quiet entrance anywhere, so she drew Edmund's attention as well as she rustled toward them in her red-trimmed evening gown. "Oh, Sir Edmund, you must be nearly freezing to death. Would you like to warm yourself by the fire before dinner? We will give you all the time you need to ready yourself."

He thanked her with a smile and nod before turning back toward Selina. It took her a moment to realize that he needed to pass her on the stairs to get to his room. She stepped aside, another wave of coldness following him as he passed her on the stairs. His eyes met hers briefly, unspoken words heavy in the air between them, before he climbed the rest of the staircase.

Selina released a slow breath, swallowing the emotion in her throat. Mama rushed forward the moment Edmund was out of sight. "Not to worry. I have a plan."

Those words combined with Mama's mischievous smile were not comforting in the slightest. But Selina summoned her courage, giving a nod as she followed Mama into the drawing room to await Edmund.

He was ready for dinner within minutes. Selina could hardly relax during the meal, wondering what Mama had in mind. Rose and Mr. Vaughan sat in silence most of the time, far from oblivious to the tension between Selina and Edmund. The conversation over the meal consisted mostly of Mama's questions directed at Edmund, none of which, thankfully, involved his feelings for Selina. There seemed to be a sort of game between Selina and Edmund. Each time she looked at him, he caught her watching, only to be caught doing the same a minute later. If Mama did not have a propensity for speaking so much, the meal would have been excruciatingly awkward.

If only Selina could read his thoughts, and if only he could read hers. Then he would know how very sorry she felt, and she wouldn't have to say all those difficult words aloud. He would know how much he meant to her. That she trusted him and loved him.

Shortly after returning to the drawing room, Mama's foot began tapping against the carpet, her eyes flitting to the longcase clock repeatedly. Rose touched Mama's elbow in an obvious attempt to calm her.

"Why are you so anxious?" Selina whispered. It was making her even more nervous.

Mama glanced to the door as Edmund and Mr. Vaughan joined them before leaning close to Selina's ear. "I asked the servants to remove themselves from the kitchen promptly by eight."

Selina frowned as she glanced up at the clock. It was one minute before the hour. "Why does that mat—"

"Oh, Sir Edmund!" Mama said, just as he took a seat. "I wondered if you might assist me with a task of tremendous importance."

Edmund's eyebrows lifted and he regarded her seriously. "Of course. What is it?"

Mama placed her hands in her lap, nearly bouncing as she turned to Selina. "Would you and Selina go to the kitchens to ensure your plum pudding is still aging well? You must test the smell and the texture by pressing softly on the outside of the wrappings. It will be served in just a few short days, you know."

Mama's intentions became quite clear, and Selina's heart flipped with nervousness. It was a ridiculous request, but Edmund still nodded, rising to his feet. With a pointed look from Mama, Selina felt much like a horse beneath a whip, and she rose quickly to her feet as well. Rose gave her an encouraging smile, and Selina pretended she didn't see it, balling her hands at her sides.

Mama waved from her place on the sofa as Selina followed Edmund to the door. He gestured for her to walk ahead of him before he stepped into the dim hallway beside her. Selina's heart pounded as she searched for the right thing to say. Daring a glance at his face, she found his eyes fixed on her.

"I am honored that your mother trusts me with a task like this," he said in a quiet voice. "Considering what she thinks happened the last time I set foot in the kitchen after dark."

A bloom of hope unfolded in Selina's chest at the small smile he cast her. His expression was still tentative, as if he were unsure if making jests was acceptable between them or not.

"That is why she asked me to accompany you," Selina said, her voice just as quiet as his. "She could not trust you alone with the pudding a second time."

Edmund's smile grew, and he looked down at the floor. His expression became more serious as they approached the kitchen door. All that weighed heavily on Selina's mind must have also weighed on his. It was difficult to laugh and smile with such a downward force pressing upon her.

When they walked inside the kitchen, it was empty, just as Mama had requested. The dishes had already been cleaned, and not another soul was there among the pots and pans and . . .

Selina squinted in the dim light until her eyes adjusted. In the far corner of the kitchen, the plum pudding had been hung in its wrappings from a hook on the ceiling.

"Shall we divide our tasks?" Selina asked when silence reigned for too long. She turned to face Edmund. Her legs shook beneath her. "I would suggest that you be responsible for smelling the pudding since you are much taller than I. And if I reach high enough, I will be able to test the texture of the pudding." Hearing the words aloud made their errand sound even more ridiculous. Could Mama not have invented a better excuse? She walked until she reached the pudding nonetheless.

Her heart thudded as Edmund moved closer to her in the dim room. "I suspect your mother had a different design in sending us here together," he said as he reached her. His gaze was careful as he studied her face.

Selina could hardly breathe, but she feigned nonchalance as she turned toward the pudding, casting a casual glance back at Edmund as she reached up to touch the side of the wrappings. She could smell the brandy, fruit, and spices on the moist fabric even from far beneath it. "Oh? What do you suppose her purpose is?" She didn't dare turn around.

"There are several possibilities," Edmund said. Why did he sound so nervous? It only made Selina's heart pound faster. "She could be planning a New Year's Day surprise for us. Or she could be so vexed with us that she wished for us to leave her sight." He moved one step closer, the sound of his boot against the floor penetrating the silence. "Or she could be hoping that I would propose to you."

Selina's eyes widened, but she pretended to still be examining the pudding, poking one side of it, then the other, careful not to make it sway too much on the hook. She rose on her toes in order to reach it. Her stomach fluttered. "I suspect the latter has been her design all along. She would have never invited you to stay if she hadn't been hoping for such a thing."

He was silent for a long moment. "Do you still wish to disappoint your mother?"

Selina shook her head before finding the strength to whisper, "No."

His boot echoed softly on the floor again before his hand wrapped around hers, pulling it away from the plum pudding. As she turned, he cupped her hand between both of his, holding it softly against his chest. She felt the steady beat of his heart against her palm, and his eyes held a sea of emotions. "Selina, I think we have misunderstood one another."

"Undoubtedly." Selina sniffed, fighting the lump in her throat.

His gaze searched hers, and he exhaled with a sigh. "When I saw you kiss Skinner I simply . . . reacted poorly. I thought that meant you loved him just as ardently as you had professed. And I did not want it to be true."

Selina's heart skipped at the hint of jealousy in his features. "Do you think when you kissed Miss Perry I didn't feel those same painful things you just described? I thought you intended to marry her after kissing her like that." Even the memory sent a jolt of ache through her heart. She scowled up at him unintentionally.

"Do you suppose *that* is how a man kisses a woman he intends to marry?" Edmund scoffed, his gaze deepening as he took a step closer. He released her hand, leaving it against his chest as he touched her face gently, tipping her chin upward. He leaned closer, his gaze falling to her lips before flicking back to her eyes. "You're wrong."

Selina could hardly breathe as she counted each beat of his heart against her hand. Was it pounding faster than it had before? Warmth spiraled through her chest as he tipped his head closer, cradling her face in his hands. His lower lip grazed over hers, sending a shiver down her neck and shoulders. Selina held onto his jacket, afraid she would fall at any moment. He drew an audible breath before his lips met hers again.

She had underestimated the value of Edmund's kiss, the effect it would have on her, the way his hands would feel against her cheeks. Already his kiss held thrice the value of Noah's. Ten times the value. Perhaps more. There was nothing the Frost Fair could have done to convince her that a reticule on the Thames was of greater value than a reticule in the shop, but Selina was quickly realizing not all kisses were equal. Not all kisses were heart-stopping and precious, rare and treasured. This . . . this was a kiss worth everything she owned. It was worth admitting every mistake, sacrificing her pride, and risking her heart. Edmund may not have been kissing her on the River Thames, but this kiss was worth more than she could ever afford.

Yet he demanded no price. He didn't want her money. The way his lips moved, fervent and slow, the way his fingers became lost in her hair, it was clear that he wanted . . . *her*.

Selina's hands curled into fists against his chest. Her heart ached with an overindulgence, much like her stomach had felt after the Christmas Day Feast. She had never felt so wanted and loved, so free of doubt and hurt. Edmund's kisses deepened as fresh tears slipped from her eyes. She clung to his jacket, pulling him closer so he might never, ever stop.

His lips parted from hers abruptly with no little amount of effort. He leaned back enough to look in her eyes, his chest rising and falling against her hands. "You must understand that my feelings for you are genuine, no matter how my attentions toward you began. They have ended like this." His voice was a hoarse whisper. "I do not wish to be parted from you when the frost melts. I love you, Selina, and I don't *ever* wish to be parted from you."

Selina closed her eyes as his words soaked through her bones, filling her with strength and warmth. "Does this mean you wish to marry me?"

"I thought my kiss would have answered that question."

"I may require a bit more proof."

Edmund smiled, leaning closer, as if he truly did mean to kiss her just as thoroughly as he had before. She stopped his lips with her thumb. "Edmund," she said in a quiet voice. There was more she still had to say. "I love you. I should have trusted you from the beginning. I cannot believe that you tolerated me for so long. I cannot believe all that you have sacrificed." Her voice broke. "Did Mr. Skinner burn your grandmother's will?"

Edmund shook his head. "He fooled me as easily as he fooled you. My grandmother did not leave her will with his father's office; he only pretended she did in order to threaten me. I learned that she intended to leave it with me, but I have searched her house these last two days to no avail."

"I will help you search." Selina stared up at him with wide eyes. "It must be somewhere, and perhaps a pair of new eyes will help discover it."

Edmund did not seem to be overly concerned with the will at that moment, his gaze sweeping over her face as he dried the moisture that remained on the edges of her eyes with his thumb. "I will accept your company anywhere I can."

"Even in an empty kitchen?" Selina cast her gaze around the room with a smile.

"Especially then." Edmund leaned close with a mischievous smile, pressing a soft kiss against her lips. His arms wrapped around her waist, and she pulled back, breathless. "I believe you have confused your traditions," she whispered before his lips captured hers again. She touched the side of his face, a laugh escaping her as his mouth parted from hers for a brief moment. She could hardly gather her words with the way he looked at her, with the feeling of his strong hands at her waist or the look of his impatient lips waiting to kiss her again. "The plum pudding is far from a kissing bough," she said.

Edmund glanced up, a slow smile spreading over his face. "Just think of how much dearer that pudding will be to your mother once she learns what has occurred beneath it. You became engaged to me."

Selina laughed. "Although I'm not certain she will approve of the kissing."

Edmund's gaze roamed her face, his smile still lingering as he brushed the curls from her forehead. "Then you may take this as your last opportunity. Once you grant her wish of having me as a son-in-law, you shall never have a chance to disappoint her again."

Selina's heart skipped as he tugged her close, stealing her breath before her laughter could escape. She kissed him with as much fervor as he kissed her, rising on her toes to bury her fingers in his hair. Edmund pulled back abruptly once more, groaning as he stepped back a pace. The restraint in his eyes reminded her of the abiding truth about the man she loved.

He was a true gentleman. Not disguised as one as Noah had been.

"It would be cruel of us to keep the news from your mother a moment longer," he said.

Selina nodded, her heart still racing with disbelief. She would marry Edmund soon. She could hardly believe she had come so close to sharing her life with anyone but him. Edmund pressed a lingering kiss to her forehead, wrapping her hand up in his. Then, hand in hand, they walked back to the drawing room.

CHAPTER 19

❄

Standing back a few paces, Edmund observed Selina tug at the ribbons of her velvet bonnet as she walked through the front doors of his grandmother's house. Even as she cast her gaze about the room, her eyes seemed incapable of missing any important detail the house contained. She had been even more eager than he had to help him search for the will the very next day. As expected, Mrs. Ellis had been overjoyed to hear of their engagement and had already begun planning how she would reveal the news to Mrs. Perry on Twelfth Night.

"Where have you not yet searched?" Selina asked, pacing the floor of the entry hall. Edmund smiled. The way she played the role of detective was vastly endearing.

"I have searched the entire house twice." Edmund felt much more at ease with the situation now that Selina was there, but there was still a piece of his heart that yearned to know what his grandmother had left for him—what pieces of her and his childhood he could keep close.

Selina walked ahead of Edmund toward the drawing room. "If you did not find the will, then you must not have searched the *entire* house. Have you spoken to the servants?"

Edmund nodded. "On two separate occasions."

Selina stopped in the middle of the drawing room, tapping her chin. Her gaze settled on the table beside his grandmother's favorite chair. A smile lit her face. "Is this the elephant statue your grandmother demanded be kept free of dust?" She bent over to examine it. "Oh, dear. I do see a bit of dust on its trunk. It seems he has been neglected during these past weeks."

Selina picked it up, blowing gently across the top of its head to clear away the dust that had settled there as well as the trunk. She used the end of her coat to clear the rest of it, smiling down at her work. "You see, Edmund, I will not be forcing you to dust my tiger statue when I am an old woman. I will do it myself."

Edmund grinned, walking closer. As he approached, Selina lowered the statue to the table. Just before the base of the elephant touched the surface, she stopped, her eyes rounding with surprise. "What is that?"

Edmund followed her gaze to the table, where a paper sat, folded in a neat square in the space where the elephant statue had been positioned.

"Could it be . . . " Selina's voice rose with excitement.

Edmund picked up the paper, his heart pounding in his throat. As he unfolded it, the writing came into view. "The will," he breathed.

Selina gave a quiet gasp.

Edmund read it over without pause, relief flooding over his shoulders. It was as he had hoped. Everything that had been acquired under his grandmother's fortune was now Edmund's.

The house. The furnishings, and even the elephant statue she had known he loved so much. He could imagine her in her final moments, holding the statue and slipping her will beneath it, knowing Edmund would find it there. He likely wouldn't have moved the statue, had Selina not been there to do so. His grandmother had been the last to place the statue there, so he hadn't dared move it.

As soon as he finished reading the document, he turned to Selina. "I do not despise London so much anymore," he said, taking her hand in his. He brushed the curls from her eyes. "If I had not come here, I would not have seen you again. And now that I know this house belongs to me, I would like to live here with you. It is a short distance from your mother, who I know will miss me severely if we venture too much farther."

Selina laughed before regarding him seriously. "I would live in a tiny cottage if it meant I could live with you. It doesn't matter where we go."

Edmund couldn't help but press a kiss to her cheek. "Would you live with me even if we could not afford a cook?"

Selina clasped her hands behind his neck, glancing upward as if deeply considering his question. "That does not matter. With my fifteen thousand, I daresay we can afford a very talented cook."

He chuckled, wrapping his arms around her waist and lifting her toes off the ground. He kissed the tip of her nose, then her lips, before setting her on the ground again. "Nonsense. I am talented enough in the kitchen," he said.

"We shall see about that at dinner on Twelfth Night." Selina raised one eyebrow. "Our talents will be put to the ultimate test."

"If Mrs. Perry approves, then we shall know that keeping a cook is unnecessary."

Selina shook her head. "Mrs. Perry will not approve of anything tomorrow with how disagreeable her mood will be when she discovers we are engaged."

Edmund gave a solemn nod. "If only the Duke of Rye were here to heartily approve."

"I daresay the Duke would be tempted enough by our pudding to devour it in his sleep."

Edmund tipped his head back with a laugh before regarding her seriously. "I only hope it is free of egg shells."

He watched her contemplative expression and the smile hovering on her lips. Her eyes hardened with determination as she looked up at him. "We shall consider the pudding a success, whether the others like it or not."

Edmund took a deep breath and smiled. "The pudding is already a success whether the others like it or not. It brought us together."

He had expected Selina to smile, or even kiss him, but she scowled instead. "Even if you were only pretending to like me that day?"

He took her hands in his, tracing his thumb over her knuckles. "I liked you all along. It was love that came unexpectedly."

A slight smile tugged on her lips. "I confess I did not even like you for a time." Edmund opened his mouth to protest, but she took a step closer, brushing his hair off his forehead with a smile. "There was something quite wrong with me then." Her voice lowered to a whisper, her round eyes gazing into his.

He hadn't ever been so affected by words, but he hung onto every one Selina spoke. He nearly laughed, or heartily agreed that there had indeed been something wrong with her, but instead he pulled her into his arms. She rested her head against his chest, and he held it there, running his fingers softly over her hair. Her arms wrapped around his shoulders, and she held him tight. He could hardly believe all that had occurred during his time in London. His shock over securing Selina's heart was still more difficult to believe than the fact that this house where they stood was now his. Theirs. He had already begun imagining the life they could build together. The laughter and the love they would share. His heart pounded as he stepped back enough to look in Selina's eyes.

"How much time does your mother require to plan your wedding?" Edmund asked.

Selina cast him a thoughtful look. "She will likely wish to wait until after the weather has warmed a bit. She will want my wedding to be unforgettable, and far more extravagant than the wedding Mrs. Perry planned for her daughter."

"If only we could marry atop the river Thames."

Selina shook her head with a laugh. "I don't wish to take a fall in my wedding gown."

He tugged her closer, interlocking his fingers behind her waist. "At least if we are married, you falling on top of me in front of a crowd will be far less scandalous."

Her cheeks reddened before she burst out laughing, covering her face with both hands. "I believe you have it all wrong," she said as she peered out from behind her fingers. "*That* was the moment that brought us together."

"Indeed," Edmund said, a fond smile stealing over his expression as he reflected on that day. "Imagine if I had not gone to the Frost Fair. I never would have seen you with Skinner."

"You never would have stopped me." Selina's voice grew solemn. "I believe you were my first Christmastide miracle, Edmund."

The sincerity in her gaze nearly made his heart stop. He stole a slow kiss from her lips before whispering close to her ear. "You were mine. You did come at the steep price of my time and effort, but I should have expected that after finding you at the Frost Fair."

She pulled away to scowl at him, but her lips twitched into an exasperated smile instead. Before she could scold him, he took one of her hands in his and adjusted his other at her waist, guiding her into a waltz. The confusion on her brow slowly faded as he began humming the song they had danced to on Christmas. Their laughter echoed in his grandmother's empty house —*their* empty house—until all traces of his humming were gone. Laughter was their new song, and there would be no final note to part them.

❄

The pudding was brought out on a silver platter, and none of the guests seemed to mind the change of tradition having it served on Twelfth Night. It wobbled slightly as it was placed at the center of the table. Selina exchanged a glance with Edmund. He sat with his shoulders back, a slight smirk of pride on his lips as the pudding was sliced and distributed to the guests. Despite not aging as long as it was meant to, the pudding still tasted of spice and fruit and all the flavors of Christmastide.

Mrs. Perry took a minuscule bite, brows drawn together with skepticism. Her doubt relented as she took her second bite, and a sigh escaped her lips. "I must agree that this is an exemplary dessert."

Mama glowed as she gave a deep nod, her gaze flicking in Selina's direction, then Edmund's. "I believe it was the love between the two who prepared it that made it so exemplary."

Rose pressed her lips together to minimize her smile. Selina tried her best to maintain an even expression. Mama had been eager to announce Selina's engagement for days, and she was bound to do so with no small amount of boasting.

Mrs. Perry's eyebrows shot up; as did her daughter's. "Love?"

Mama laughed, touching her necklace with one delicate finger. "Oh, I must have forgotten to tell you the news."

"News?" Mrs. Perry swallowed visibly.

"Sir Edmund has proposed to my Selina, and they are to be wed very soon." Mama took another bite of her plum pudding, closing her eyes as she savored it. "Oh, yes, this was made with a great deal of love, indeed." When she opened her eyes, they shone with victory.

Miss Perry did not seem quite as disappointed as her mother, but rather relieved. A smile stole over her lips as she continued eating in silence. Perhaps her pursuit of Edmund had only been motivated by her mother's expectations. Mrs. Perry's nostrils flared, and she stabbed her pudding with her fork. "Ah, I offer my sincerest congratulations." She offered a smile to Edmund, then Selina, before hiding her clenched teeth behind her lips. After taking another bite of the pudding, she cleared her throat. "Despite its flaws, I suppose I see how the Duke could have liked this dish."

Mama raised her eyebrows. "*Flaws?*"

As the polite bickering commenced, Selina met Edmund's

gaze across the table. She could hardly do so without laughing, so she returned her attention to her plate, finishing every last crumb of the plum pudding. Edmund seemed just as surprised as she was to find that it was delicious and that there was not a single egg shell to be found.

After the ladies returned to the drawing room, Edmund, Mr. Perry, and Mr. Vaughan stayed back for their port. It would be several minutes before they joined the ladies. Selina bounced her foot impatiently as she waited for Edmund to return to her side. A smile already pulled on her lips at the thought of the events of dinner they had yet to discuss. Selina couldn't remember a happier Twelfth Night, nor could she imagine a better way to spend every Christmastide than with Edmund at her side.

She had never imagined that love could be so gripping, enough to keep her toes bouncing on the rug until Edmund returned, to keep her mind spinning with a flurry of hope for the future. At first she was surprised that Edmund had stolen her heart, and she was even more surprised that she had stolen his. But love was never something to be understood; it was something to be felt and treasured, and Selina had learned it had a proclivity for surprises.

But as Edmund walked through the drawing room door, dark curls falling over his brow and a broad smile on his lips, she was not surprised at all to find that his gaze fell on her first.

AUTHOR'S NOTE

Thank you for reading! I hope you enjoyed Edmund and Selina's love story, and that it brought a smile to your face. Along with the other four authors involved in this series, I thoroughly enjoyed researching the Frost Fair, which was a real event in history. In February of the year 1814, the Thames did freeze over, and a fair was held on the surface, just as we describe in our stories! For the sake of our Christmas theme, we fictionalized the dates of the fair to fit our timeline, but the events of the fair remain the same. I hope you enjoyed learning about such an interesting event in this book, and I hope you will read the others to come in the series!

JOIN THE NEWSLETTER

SIGN UP HERE!
Stay tuned to receive updates about Ashtyn Newbold's latest works!

FOLLOW THE AUTHOR ON SOCIAL MEDIA
FACEBOOK.COM/AUTHORASHTYN

INSTAGRAM.COM/ASHTYN_NEWBOLD_AUTHOR

MORE BOOKS BY ASHTYN NEWBOLD

Larkhall Letters Series
Book 1: The Ace of Hearts
Book 2: The Captain's Confidant

Brides of Brighton Series
A Convenient Engagement
Marrying Miss Milton
Romancing Lord Ramsbury
Miss Weston's Wager
An Unexpected Bride

Standalone novels
The Last Eligible Bachelor
An Unwelcome Suitor
Mischief and Manors
Lies and Letters
Road to Rosewood

Novellas & Anthologies
The Earl's Mistletoe Match
The Midnight Heiress
Unexpected Love

ABOUT THE AUTHOR

Ashtyn Newbold grew up with a love of stories. When she discovered chick flicks and Jane Austen books in high school, she learned she was a sucker for romantic ones. When not indulging in sweet romantic comedies and regency period novels (and cookies), she writes romantic stories of her own across several genres. Ashtyn also enjoys baking, singing, sewing, and anything that involves creativity and imagination.

Connect with Ashtyn Newbold on these platforms!
ashtynnewbold.com

Printed in Great Britain
by Amazon